SKY LOVE
A SKY INK NOVEL BOOK 1

T. M. DAWSON

To Pat Fish for allowing me the use of one of her tattoos for this book and fictional family. For my mom and dad, and for Sharae Davis for listening to me when I talked about the book incessantly. To Rand Lees for believing in me. To Aimee Shaye, and her husband for the cover and my editor Angel Nyx. Thanks to everyone! You can find Pat Fish's work at luckyfishart.com. She is a great tattoo artist that specializes in Celtic. Thanks Pat! I hope to see you soon and get to add these tattoos as my own!

Copyright © 2021 by T.M. Dawson
All rights reserved. No part of this publication may be reproduced, distributed, translated, or transmitted in any form or by any means, including photocopying, recording, or other electronic or mechanical methods, without the prior written permission of the publisher, except in the case of brief quotations embodied in critical reviews and certain other noncommercial uses permitted by copyright law. For permission requests, send me a message.
Please do not reproduce or copy any of my work. This is a work of fiction and any resemblance to any person or place, is purely coincidence.

❀ Created with Vellum

CHAPTER ONE

ANNALISE KNEW SHE SHOULDN'T HAVE MESSED WITH A MONEY tycoon, but Joseph Declan seemed like the perfect partner. Everything about him seemed like all of her dreams had come true. The book, the sexy man with connections to publishers, and her dad, James O'Callaghan, one of the world's richest men. Annalise definitely thought then that being the daughter of James O'Callaghan, and the fiancé to Joseph, was a grand thing. Annalise learned after she began writing her book that rich Annalise was a spoiled brat. Annalise would have rather been the Annalise that worked on her own way to a good life.

When Annalise talked to Joseph about it, he exploded. Apparently he wanted a trophy wife. She looked at the tickets in her hand and pursed her lips. Was it a bad thing that she was running?

Annalise shook her head it was better to leave and start a new life and a new career as an author. She handed the flight attendant my ticket, and boarded the plane, and that's when she saw him, her seat partner.

He was tall, muscular under his tight sweater. When he turned to her, he smiled, showing straight white teeth.

"Looks like we're buddies," Annalise told him.

"You first," he said in a thick Scottish accent.

Annalise shook her head. "I don't ride by the windows."

He nodded and scooted into the seat by the window. He was fast asleep an hour later when she pulled her laptop out, opening her book and started writing. Annalise looked at her buddy as he slept. He was handsome, and he held a tan very well, unlike her. What was his name? Was he from Scotland? Annalise shook her head at that last question. *Of course he is from Scotland, you idiot!* She was glad he wasn't awake or her blush would be an indicator that she was thinking about him.

The plane shook with some turbulence, the captain said, and Annalise took in a breath of air and held it. *Oh god, oh god.* Why did it have to be a freaking plane! She felt a warm hand on hers, and she turned to find her plane buddy holding it and smiling at her.

"Just a bunch of wind is all. Don't fret, now breathe before you cause yourself to faint," he told her and she relaxed and let out the breath she had been holding.

"What's your name?" Annalise asked him an hour later as she worked.

"Lachlan, and you?"

"Annalise."

Lachlan smiled. Annalise went back to her work, not wanting him to see how much his smile, green eyes, and handsome face got to her. She was pretty, but not beautiful by any means, and she doubted he felt the way she did when she stared at him. *What is this stalker central? Your acting lovesick and you barely know the man.* Another hour passed, and Lachlan was back to sleep beside her. Whatever he did for a living must be tiring. The rest of the flight went by without a word from either until Scotland when Lachlan said his goodbye.

Her dad was waiting with his driver by his limo, smoking a cigarette when Annalise walked out of the airport. They both fought over opening the door until the driver relented. Dad didn't like being waited on hand and foot, that wasn't his style even though he was a very important person. That's just how it worked. Annalise climbed into the back seat. Dad put out his cigarette and followed.

"How was the flight, Dove?" he asked, using his nickname for her.

"It was alright," Annalise told him, not mentioning Lachlan keeping her calm for part of the flight. She didn't like to bare her emotions to him, it felt weak.

Dad nodded and quickly pulled his phone out as a call came through. One to be working. He had to take this call. Annalise looked out the window as buildings passed her. It was definitely different from Seattle; she hadn't remembered just how different it could be. Hopefully, it rejuvenated the muse and kept her far away from Joseph. She hadn't blocked him from her phone yet, but she also knew he likely would not be texting or calling.

Dad hung up the phone and turned to her. "You'll be staying at the mansion."

"Why do I have to stay there? I can just get my place."

"Because I want you to stay. I need someone watching the place and helping with the upcoming parties. I can't be in two places at once," he explained to her.

"So I am to be the hostess to these parties? What about my book? I am on deadline, Dad."

"I thought of that, and I also thought that you should take a break. I am not ready to approve the book, Joseph might find you here and I want you safe."

"Approve my book? You're not my ed—Oh no, you bought the damn publishing house, didn't you?"

Dad nodded and gave her a deep smile. "I bought it for you. It was a surprise, and I blew it. We are building a new one here in Scotland. That was a surprise too, I am two for two today. Sorry, a lot on my mind."

"You can't keep doing this, every time I have come close to getting this book published and you just keep on finding excuses for me not finishing it. Dad, I am going to finish and publish this book and there is nothing you can do or say."

Dad nodded. "Thought you might say that, okay Dove, if that's what you want. But we need to not give information out, I want you safe, so for now no blurb with your whereabouts. Deal?"

Annalise sighed. "Deal."

Annalise dumped her bags in the room that she grew up in. It was an enormous room, with a California queen sized bed, chandelier, multiple wardrobes, and a big walk-in closet. The room was filled with her high school stuff, and multiple pictures with her mom and dad when her mom had been alive, and they'd lived in Seattle. Annalise smiled as she took a picture of her mom from the corkboard next to her desk. Mom had been beautiful, with long red hair, and beautiful green eyes and freckles on her skin. Sometimes, she had talked Dad into going out for the night to Paris, or to Egypt for a weekend. She'd been an extravagant spender, and an obsessed reader of books. Before she'd met Dad, she had been a travel writer. That was the reason Annalise wanted to be an author.

Annalise wiped the tears from her face. Mom was killed in their apartment in Seattle, exactly one month after Dad and her divorced. There had been no leads, and the case had grown cold. Annalise put the picture back on the desk. It was a memory she rarely let herself remember because she had been the one to find her that day after school. Annalise shook her head to rid herself of the memory and unpacked her things. She would finish here and go for a jog before she had to hit the keyboard.

CHAPTER TWO

A WEEK LATER, ANNALISE WATCHED AS PEOPLE ARRIVED. She turned on her heel and out into the large mansion where the guests that danced and talked in the giant room her dad was using for a ballroom. Fancy parties, that was what James O' Callaghan known for, other than his net worth. They would throughout Skye. It was a great turnout, Dad would be pleased. Now, if Dad had stayed at the party.

She looked through the crowd and smiled when she saw a familiar face within the crowd. A certain handsome Scotsman she'd met on the plane a week earlier. Annalise descended the stairs, and moved through the enormous crowd before following him out the back patio and outside among the garden. There, he looked at the flowers, adjusting his kilt. He probably wore nothing underneath it. She giggled like a schoolgirl and startled him. When he turned around, he caught his leg on an angel statue and fell into the rosebush.

Annalise rushed over to help him, and when she saw his handsome face up close, she smiled. He was so incredibly handsome up close.

"I'm so sorry, Lachlan," Annalise said.

"No, no, it's fine." He looked at her and realization dawned in his eyes.

"Your name was Lachlan, right?"

"Aye, it is," he said as he got his balance back. He smiled, showing perfect white teeth. "Didn't think I would see you again."

"I didn't either," she said looking him up and down. "So, a kilt?"

Lachlan looked down at the kilt he wore. "Oh, this? Well, I thought to dress the same way the actors looked. Mr. O'Callaghan went all out in tradition with this party. So, Macleod family clan colors."

"Well, you didn't have too. My dad likes to make a big deal about his parties. The actors inside are not from any clans I know.

"Well, if he wanted true Scots, he didn't have to go far," Lachlan said and then did a double take. "Wait a minute, you are James O'Callaghans daughter?"

Annalise's lips thinned. *Cat's out of the bag now.*

"Wouldn't have known you certainly don't take after him," Lachlan said.

"I am glad of that. I only got his hair and eyes, and his sharp mind. I wouldn't want to be his exact twin. "So, what exactly are you doing here?" Annalise asked. "I doubt you're here to be an actor double."

"Oh no, I am here with my family," Lachlan said.

"You're married?"

"Of course not, I am here with my da, ma, and my brother. Da knows your father, they go way back."

"Really? I didn't know that. But Dad never really talks about his friends," Anneliese explained.

"So, are you playing the beautiful hostess?" Lachlan asked.

Annalise nodded. "They trapped me into it, believe me, I'd rather be upstairs writing."

"Oh, you're an author, what do you write?"

"Paranormal Romance, sometimes contemporary," Anneliese replied. "Right now, I am working on a paranormal romance. Still in the plotting stage."

Lachlan smiled, he loved hearing her talk. It was like sweet music to his ears. He felt his face warm.

"What's wrong?" Anneliese asked him.

Lachlan cleared his throat. "Chilly is all."

Gods, she caused him to feel like a school lad just learning about girls. If she did that to him, what else could that smile, and her voice, do to him? She might just be his downfall from grace.

Anneliese smiled. "Would you like to get a drink with me, Lachlan?"

"I would." He put his arm out for Annalise to hold on to. "My Lady."

Annalise giggled and allowed Lachlan to walk her inside. They settled at a table close to the band with their drinks.

"So, what made you come to Scotland?" Lachlan asked as he drank.

Annalise swallowed. "Visiting my dad."

"And your book?"

"Needed a change of pace."

Lachlan nodded, he couldn't't help but think that Annalise was hiding something, but it wasn't his place to ask her.

"What about you, do you live close?"

Lachlan nodded. "I live on Skye."

"Really?" Annalise leaned forward. "I've been wanting to visit. I've lived here for a longtime and never been to Skye."

"You've lived here before?"

"Mm hm. When I was a girl."

"Really, I would have thought you'd have a thick accent."

Annalise laughed. "Not as thick as yours, but I can try if you really want to hear it." She cleared her throat. "Aye, we're in a bit of a fankle."

Lachlan laughed. "That was actually pretty good."

Annalise smiled. "Thank you, thank you, everyone."

Lachlan smiled wider. But it was short-lived. He looked past Annalise, a slight frown on his handsome face. Annalise followed his gaze and watched as a drop dead gorgeous blonde walked toward them.

Lachlan stood. "Excuse me."

He made his way over to the blonde and talked to her. He grabbed her arm, and they left. Annalise pursed her lips and downed her drink. The party was winding down finally, and the last of the stragglers were already leaving. In a matter of minutes, the house was silent, and Jackson and Maggie, her father's butler and maid, locked up for the night.

Annalise made her way upstairs, and to her room. She sat down at her desk and opened her book. If Lachlan wanted to be rude and go off with the blonde, let him! She put her head in her hands and wiped her face vigorously. Why was she even bothered by this? She barely knew the man. Writing would be her retreat from that, maybe then she could forget about it all.

Annalise worked until she got sucked into her book. She was on a roll; the anger fueling her to play with her characters. Annalise finished at midnight, her anger finally spent. She stretched and stood. Finally, she could go to bed, happy that the book was heading in the right direction. Annalise climbed into her bed and fell asleep as soon as her head hit the pillow.

CHAPTER THREE

Lachlan Macleod slammed another shot glass down in front of his younger brother Kieran Macleod and gave a triumphant laugh. Kieran growled and motioned for another round. The two brothers stared at each other, unaware of the crowed they had caused and downed the drinks. Lachlan came out the winner once more and laughed as his brother banged his fist on their table.

"Enough," Their dad, Murdoch Macleod, said as he strode up to the two young men, their mother Cassie next to him nursing a glass of Guinness. "You'll both fall under the table and I won't be dragging ye home."

"Aw Da, one more drink," slurred Kieran and he laughed and pointed at Lachlan. "Drinks."

Lachlan laughed with a shake of his head. "No, Da is right, ye've had enough. No more for ye." He motioned to the barkeep to cut them off and laid a few bills on the table for their server. "Let's get ye home, aye?"

Lachlan stood and helped his little brother up, propping his arm over one shoulder and walking him to the door of the bar their parents following close behind. They passed by a table of young women, and Kieran halted and looked at them with a drunk smile on his handsome, sharp features.

"What's yer name pretties?" he slurred, and the girls looked at each other trying not to laugh.

"Yer drunk ye fud," Lachlan told him and turned to the women. "Pardon my brother, he cannot hold his liquor."

"I am not drunks," Kieran said, and the girls laughed. He scowled at them. "Its nots funny."

"Keep telling yourself that, brother of mine." The women laughed again, and Lachlan ushered his brother out of the bar and into the car where he promptly passed out. Lachlan looked at his parents. "Well, I can say he'll have need of hair of the dog tomorrow."

Murdoch chuckled, then sobered at the look his wife threw his way. "We will take him home son, ye need a ride?"

"No, I can walk from here." Lachlan hugged his mom and dad and began walking down the street away from the bar.

The Isle of Skye
Annalise's Cottage

Annalise stood in the kitchen of her newly furnished and bought cottage on the Isle of Skye. It was a beautiful cottage with brick walls and hardwood floors and with a library she could work out of and a second floor where three bedrooms, each with their own bathroom, sat. When Jordan had pulled up to the cottage, she'd been pleased to find it had a small garden with small daffodils and roses growing in it. She would plant more flowers, in a variety of colors. She also found her blue sedan she had owned in Seattle sitting in the driveway polished and looking like the day she'd gotten it.

Jordan walked into the kitchen with a warm smile. "Beautiful, isn't it?"

Annalise looked at him and laughed. "Yes, and big too. I wasn't expecting a house."

"James didn't think you would want to live with him and figured you would be more comfortable in a home of your own."

Annalise smiled, she'd lived with her dad once before and it had removed them from one another. One or the other person in different rooms, no she could never do that again.

"Dad was right in buying this place. Tell him I am happy with it."

Jordan bowed and left her alone in her kitchen. Annalise twirled around her kitchen with a squeal, her kitchen! She had a tiny one room efficiency in Seattle. Now, she had a big cottage overlooking the village of Portree and a chance that few people get to have. Annalise walked from her kitchen to her living room and marveled at the extra space she hadn't had living in her simple efficiency.

A fireplace sat against the wall before her. To her right, a small bar that gave a small glimpse into her kitchen and a small space behind it to allow for a small dining table. To her left was a small space for a T.V. and before the fireplace a small couch. She would make it cozy, set up her couch so that it would get all the warmth of the fire in the fireplace, and also give whoever was sitting on it the advantage of watching the T.V. without being too warm.

Annalise turned and walked out of the door behind her and into the hallway leading to the stairs to her upper floor. Annalise had a small space in the corner; she could put a bookcase there, or a table and a small Tiffany lamp to give it a homey feel. Annalise walked up the stairs to the upper floor, there were three bedrooms up here, opening the first bedroom she found it to be small, and almost kid like.

Annalise smiled, she'd make this into her art room for it gave her an excellent view of the village, and the misty mountains beyond. She would put in an easel, and a desk suited for her drawings and a computer so that she might paint on it using the various software programs she owned, all while enjoying a beautiful scene.

She walked out of her art room and into the second bedroom. It was a little roomier than the first bedroom, and twin double doors led to a small balcony that overlooked the same image from the first bedroom. This, she decided, would be her guest room. She'd set it up so that dad could stay with her while he was traveling, and for friends who came to visit her in Scotland. That is if she still had friends after Joseph and Elspeth were done tarnishing her name. *Serves you right for dating your boss.* Annalise cursed her conscience. Could it not let her be happy?

Annalise continued to look around the room; in one corner was a large walk-in closet, and a smaller one beside it. She peered inside and envisioned a bathroom in its place. She'd have to confirm it with Dad, and then talk to her landlord but she didn't think that would be a problem. The cottage was relatively new anyway. Dad had made sure that she didn't live in one of the older cottages. Those were a part of history and should stay unchanged as little as possible. Besides, when her dad paid the last payment on the cottage the deed would be hers, and then she could do with it anyway she pleased.

Annalise walked to the last room and opened the door and squealed, jumping up and down. Her bedroom was enormous! Bigger than the other two, it sported a walk-in closet, a queen-size bed which Dad had specially ordered for her and a desk with a new laptop and desktop computer upon it, complete with a printer. Annalise took the attached a note to the screen from Dad which read:

May this find you through your hard times, I love you Annalise.

Dad, she smiled at the note and walked into the bathroom and her mouth fell open. He had gone too far in here, and had added more room into the bathroom for a walk-in shower, vanity and a Jacuzzi and a privacy toilet complete with a small door, just as she liked it. It had everything she had ever wanted in her dream bathroom. Annalise walked over to the Jacuzzi and the window that sat over it, and gasped.

In the distance stood Eilean Donan Castle, and a large cottage by a large lake, no the Scots called them lochs, she reminded herself. It sat just beyond a field on the left, although it was far away she could see it clearly. She walked into the walk-in shower and was pleased to find that the cottage and the castle could be seen from here as well. She would have to remember to call her dad and thank him for this. She didn't think she deserved such a pretty room or bathroom. She certainly didn't believe she deserved to have this pretty view.

Annalise left the bathroom and went back downstairs. Once in the kitchen, she found non-perishables in the cabinet but no other groceries in the house. No matter, she'd just go to the store and buy what she needed with the card her dad had given her, and then come home and probably sit in her Jacuzzi with a good book and a glass of wine while she contemplated her next drawing or the next book in her Sisters of the Wild series. She slung her purse over her shoulder, closed the door behind her, and walked to her car.

CHAPTER FOUR

DORNIE, SCOTLAND

EILEAN DONAN CASTLE

"So you didn't ask her for her number, just wished her well and just hoped you would meet again?" Kieran asked Lachlan as they stood at the entrance of Eilean Donan Castle one rare warm morning.

The two young men were in full regalia for the vacationing visitors, swords strapped to their bare backs. Every so often the two of them jovially quipped at each other in a Scottish burr that no one around besides their fellow Scotsmen understood.

"Well?" Kicran asked as he stretched his shoulders, repositioning his sword.

"Well, what?" Lachlan asked, and Kieran raised a dark eyebrow, his lightning blue eyes blinking, flashing with a hint of annoyance they always had. "No, I did not ask for her number and she lives on Skye. We will meet again."

"You hope." Kieran shook his head. "I would have taken her number, then asked her to dinner, and she'd have been in my bed in a flash."

"Aye and gone out of your life too, no doubt." Lachlan sighed.

"Not true, there is still Lillian. She and I have been going together for almost a month!"

Lachlan gave his brother a skeptical look and a wry grin.

"Aye your right, not going to last," Kieran said, throwing his arms in the air. "I should just cut my losses now and be done with it."

Lachlan chuckled and smiled at a little girl passing by them with her family. She pointed and her mother scooted her along. He looked around at Eilean Donan castle. He and Kieran had been coming to the place since they were children. The castle itself was on its own island in the western highlands of Scotland and surrounded by three lochs: Loch Duich, Loch Long, and Loch Alsh. It was 107,639 square feet, and boasted a ticket office, coffee shop, and gift shop.

A long bridge connected the castle to the outside world where visitors entered the castle on tours all throughout the day. The village of Dornie, where his parents lived wasn't too far, and a ferry to the Isle of Skye was in Glenelg or via the bridge at Kyle of Lochalsh eight miles from the castle. Home and the tattoo shop he ran with his brother, Skye Ink, was not too far from him.

Kieran had worked at Eilean Donan when he had turned nineteen, and Lachlan had followed his younger brother, hoping to earn extra cash to raise the funds he needed to build and fund Skye Ink. The shop was now the biggest and most well-known tattoo shop in Scotland, and was nearing its twelfth year of being open.

Lachlan smiled to himself. It had taken him and Kieran a long time to build the shop, and now that it was standing, the three of them had been bringing in the money they needed to live comfortably. In fact, Lachlan had hoped to have a new shop opened in the United States, and had even gone to Seattle where he and Kiera, and their little sister, Riley, studied full time at Gallaudet.

Sure, he could add onto the shop he had now, but what fun would that be when he could build another? Maybe even open a small gallery and bring in tattoo artists from around the world and feature their work both on canvas and in the flesh. Lachlan stared at the bridge, and his world slowed when he spotted Annalise O'Callaghan standing on it looking over the bridge, and into the loch. He smiled and turned to his brother, tapping him on the shoulder.

"I told you I would see her again."

Kieran followed his brother's gaze to the female standing on the bridge leading to the castle. She looked into the loch, her long blonde highlighted brown hair blowing in the soft spring wind. She was not skinny, nor was she chubby, but average weight with curves and ample breasts. From this distance he could see she had wide hips and didn't have to guess that her skin would be slightly tanned cream with a few freckles. No wonder Lachlan liked her. The woman was a dream.

"Well, go to her you fud!" Kieran pushed his older brother, and Lachlan chuckled and walked towards the bridge.

Wow! Such a big and pretty castle! Annalise thought as she had pulled up to the castle and walked the bridge. The loch below was pretty as well, she'd hate to fall in as she had no doubts that it was cold as hell down there. Annalise looked up and a rush of excitement sped through her as she watched

Lachlan Macleod striding towards her with a bright smile on his handsome, sharp, slightly unshaven face. He was bare chested and dressed in Macleod tartan colors, complete with fly plaid and a sword strapped to his bare back. A black tattoo, Celtic in design, wove itself from the front of his right shoulder to his bicep and disappeared to wrap to the back of his shoulder. She smiled at him as he walked towards her and raised her hand to wave when a woman walking by elbowed her in her side with a hiss. The woman's face was pale and blood-red lips curved into a wicked smile. Annalise backed against the bridge edge. She waved her arms trying to catch herself as she lost balance and toppled over the side, into the loch's icy waters. She heard a woman's screams overhead as she plummeted beneath the icy waters of Loch Alsh.

Lachlan broke into a run just as Annalise fell, unstrapping his sword and called out to Kieran, as he jumped over the ledge and into the water a few feet from Annalise, and swam towards her. He grabbed her as she crested the water. Annalise coughed up water and turned toward Lachlan as he grabbed her and clung to him. He brushed her wet hair from her face and looked into her ocean blue eyes. Annalise had never been so happy to see a man than she was Lachlan Macleod. The highlander's hard, warm body chilled her cold one and his strong-muscled arms kept her afloat so she wouldn't sink.

"Are you alright, lass?" he asked.

"Y-yes." Annalise said through chattering teeth.

"Can you hold on to me?"

Annalise nodded and swam around Lachlan as he turned in the water, and climbed onto his back and wrapped her arms around his muscular neck. She focused on his tattoo as he began to swim; it was blacker when the water touched it. Now that she was closer, she saw the Celtic knots wrapped around themselves from the back of his shoulder to the front and down to his bicep where a crest sat with the words 'Hold Fast' in blue gothic print, a small Celtic band wrapped under it around his bicep and seemed to be never-ending. It was bold, yet beautiful and fitting. Her teeth chattered and she shook from head to toe as he swam. Was Lachlan really naked underneath that kilt? She could feel his buttocks under her thighs, and she felt the cold. It was supposed to be spring for God's sake!

His brother pulled helped pull them ashore. Once they were out of the water, Lachlan grabbed onto Annalise and pulled her into his arms. She didn't fight him, just tried not to think about the warmth that suddenly pooled between her thighs. He seemed angry. Lachlan carried her into the gift shop, and the elderly woman manning the register ran from behind the counter and into the back room and returned a moment later with a towel.

"Here you are, lass, dry up." The woman handed Annalise the towel, which Lachlan grabbed and wrapped around her when he set her on her feet.

He told the elderly woman he would take her to the back and carried her through the door the woman had come from and into a small break room. He sat her into a chair and walked to a small cabinet.

"Are you angry with me?" Annalise asked as she stood.

Lachlan turned holding a tin, his handsome face grim. "No, I am not angry with you."

"Then what's wrong?" she asked.

Lachlan slammed the tin onto the counter making her jump, and in a blink of an eye he was standing right in front of her his nose to hers, his wild green eyes to her ocean blue ones. Before she could stop him, he pushed her to the door and crushed her lips with his own. Annalise moaned, and Lachlan licked her lips, coaxing her to open them so he could explore her mouth with his tongue. She opened her lips with a sigh. He dipped his tongue in and grabbed her around her waist, wrapping her legs around his hips. He ground against her, the ridge of his cock brushing against her, letting her know just how hard she made him. Annalise wrapped her arms around his neck and moaned as he grinded against her. She reached under his kilt and found his hard cock. Holy crap! He wore nothing underneath that heavy fabric! Lachlan hissed and broke the kiss.

"Easy, lass," he said huskily as she stroked him. "Easy." He kissed her once more and was about to lay her down onto the break room table when a fist pounded on the door and Kieran's voice came through.

He cursed and put her down, gently pulling her hand from his cock and adjusting his kilt.

"Yeah!"

Kieran opened the door and poked his hand inside. "The boss wants to know if the girl is okay, and to tell you to give her a free ticket to Eilean Donan." He looked at her and gave her a perverted grin. "What were you two up too?"

Lachlan lunged at his brother, and Kieran ran off with a laugh. He turned back to Annalise. "I apologize, lass."

"I-I understand, I think I should go home now." Annalise looked down at her hands. "I am sorry too." She looked at him and stared at his lips. Lachlan was doing the same. All he wanted to do was kiss her again, then bury himself deep inside her and never leave.

Annalise turned and ran out before they could do something they both would regret. Lachlan growled and ran to catch up to her just as she finished crossing the bridge and got to her car. Lachlan watched as she patted herself down for her keys and her frustrated sigh when she couldn't't find them.

"Do you need help, lass?"

"I can't find my keys, I think I lost them in the loch," Annalise said. She sniffled and Lachlan panicked.

No, no. she would not cry! He strode over to her just as she burst out in tears and pulled her into his arms, laying her head onto his broad chest as she cried. She was cold, exhausted and getting hungry. She wanted to go home and be away from these damn people and likely him. He felt guilty for lunging at her and nearly having sex with her on the break room table.

"We will get you another key, lass, but first let's get you to Miss Maggie so you can get warm." He rubbed her back and walked her towards his car, turning back to Kieran as he walked toward them. "I am going to take her to Miss Maggie, aye!"

"Aye!" Kieran called back.

Lachlan led her to a blue sedan and helped her into it, then climbed into the driver's seat.

"Dornie isn't too far from here, we can get you some clean warm clothes there from Miss Maggie," Lachlan told her as he drove away from Eilean Donan Castle and onto the A87 highway.

Lachlan looked at her. "Unless you want me to drive you home instead?"

"My house keys were with my car keys," Annalise told him, wiping her eyes, and looked out the window as they drove to Dornie.

Who was this man who had nearly had sex with her in a break room and then help her without a thought to what had just occurred between them? No one you could trust, Annalise. He is not for you and you know it. Annalise screwed her eyes shut to ward off that last thought although, she knew it was true. Lachlan Macleod was likely not the type of man that would give her a future, nor did he seem the type to date a girl. He was, she was sure, a man who slept with the ladies and moved on to the next willing woman. He'd shown that back in the break room hadn't he? Annalise swallowed the hard lump that formed in her throat, and closed her eyes and drifted off into sleep, her mind was a whir with emotions that she longed to express, and had sworn she never would again.

CHAPTER FIVE

Lachlan sat at Miss Maggie O'Connell's kitchen table. He stared up at the stairs the elderly woman had taken Annalise up thirty minutes ago. He dug his hand through his long black hair and tried to ignore the chill in the air from Maggie's constant running air conditioner. Honestly, the woman could be in the middle of a harsh Scottish winter and that damned thing would still be running. Hot natured, she was.

Lachlan stood, and would have followed the women upstairs but Maggie appeared at the top of the stairs wagging her finger as she descended.

"You're a naughty one, Lachlan Macleod," she scolded and smacked him on one of his cheeks when she dismounted the stairs in front of him. "I'll have no perverts in my home, you hear?"

Lachlan rolled his eyes and sat back in his chair. "I am frigid woman."

Maggie bustled around in her kitchen, grabbing her kettle and tea tin, then to the sink.

"You should have brought a change of clothes lad, I've no

sons." She placed the kettle on the stove and looked at him with a mischievous smile. "You could wear one of Marina's dresses, I am sure she would not mind sharing with you, although with your wide shoulders I would need to draw one out for you to fit nicely."

"Lovely old woman, maybe a nice crown of flowers to go with it aye?" Lachlan snorted crossing his arms. "Turn on the heat at least, it's fucking freezing in here."

Maggie let forth a phlegmy cackle, and Lachlan shivered. "You've a foul mouth boy, my home and my rules. I will not tolerate foul words, and you can keep your knickers on about the cool air, besides you could easily warm yourself up. Find a blanket, or wear the dress."

Lachlan's eyes narrowed. "I'll wait, and if Annalise isn't finished yet, I will leave her here to stay with you and Marina for the night."

"I am done." Annalise's voice floated down the stairs.

Lachlan turned and looked at her, and his heart slowed. Maggie chuckled but tried to cover it with a cough. Annalise flowed down the stairs wearing a blue dress that hugged her curved body and plump chest. Her long brunette and gold-highlighted hair was piled high on her head in a claw clip which was scooped to show her beautiful face and ocean blue eyes. She wore no make-up, her face was completely clean and required none. He shifted in his chair and prayed that he wasn't tenting in his kilt.

Lachlan stood, pushing his chair back hard as he crossed over to Annalise, his cheeks warm. He turned to Maggie. "I am going to shower, mind if you put my kilt on the line to dry?"

Maggie waved at him as she cooked her tea. Annalise looked up at him and met his wild green eyes. He moved closer until his bare chest was against hers, and she shivered.

Lachlan pushed passed her and up the stairs. Annalise sat

down on the chair Lachlan had vacated and placed her hand over her heart. Maggie put a cup down in front of her, making her jump.

"No need to fret dear, all those Macleod boys get a woman's knickers into a twist." The older woman sat on the chair in front of her. "Why I remember when Murdoch met Cassie, lots of sparks that sent their clothing into a blaze that day."

"Murdoch? Cassie?" Annalise asked.

"Lachlan's ma and da. Very nice family, the Macleod's, and very protective of their little ones and the men their women." Maggie smiled and looked up the stairs where Lachlan had gone.

Annalise took a sip of her tea and found it pleasantly sweet. "Are they all like that?"

"Like what my dear?"

Annalise felt her cheeks warm. "So big, and you know….Full of sex appeal."

Maggie let forth a laugh. "Oh, The Macleod's are full of that and more lassie. Don't be afraid dear, a Macleod man will knock your socks off but never hurt you with sex, you have found a fine man in Lachlan Macleod."

Annalise nodded and drank some more of her tea. Lachlan Macleod wasn't her man, would never be her man, and he was so definitely not going to use that sex appeal on her. The break room had been one step too far, and she intended it to stop there.

"Oh, I see," Maggie said and Annalise looked at her. Maggie gave her a grim smile. "I thought you and Lachlan were together."

"Why would you think that?"

"Why the way he looks at you, my dear, a man has a way he looks at his woman and means to keep her." Maggie took a sip of tea. "But if you aren't together, I am sure there are other ways a man keeps a woman. You aren't doing that with the young Macleod, are you?"

"God, no!" Annalise scowled. What was she, a whore? The only man she'd ever slept with before in any relationship was Joseph, and that had been a mistake. Again, what had happened in the break room was not going as far as that. "I would never do that with Lachlan, I mean it's perfectly healthy, but I need a relationship with flowers and hearts and puppies before I do that."

Maggie laughed and patted her hand gently. "Of course you do, I didn't mean to upset you. It's just that in this day and age women are too quick to lie with a man than when I was a young'un. I see men befriend a woman and then bed her and break her heart. I just don't want that happening to you, dear. A woman has to protect herself."

"It won't Maggie, I promise." She swore it would never happen, never again. Joseph had been the last, and she would not let Lachlan get her alone again. "Lachlan is just a friend."

Maggie nodded, and Annalise swore that the older woman's eyes seemed to see right through her.

Lachlan stood naked at the top of the stairs. Eavesdropping was rude and an action that his mother would have beat him for if she'd found out about it, but he'd simply had to hear Annalise's voice once more before he climbed into the scalding water. So, she only wanted to be his friend and no more? He wouldn't allow it. What he'd felt in the break room was something else. She had that spark, and made his heart race every time he saw her, he'd win her for himself and would be damned if he'd allow any other man have her. He'd show her he could take care of her and treat her right. He only had to find out just who had hurt her and right the wrongs that bastard had done to her.

He turned and walked into the bathroom and climbed into the shower, allowing the warm water to flow over his taut body. He'd seduce her, love her, and shower her with gifts and she'd be his. He'd fight for her and die for her if he could. He swore it. Now he'd have to get her alone to accomplish it. After their steamy incident in the break room at Eilean Donan, Annalise would likely make excuses so that she wouldn't be caught alone with him and Maggie had told Annalise all those things downstairs because he'd been listening. The old bat always knew when someone was eavesdropping. She was helping him but also giving him her answer. She would not help him, he was on his own. And so Lachlan Macleod lost his heart that day in the home of Maggie O'Connell to Annalise O'Callaghan and it prepared him to win her come hell or high water.

CHAPTER SIX

Another late night last night, Lachlan cursed as he opened Skye Ink that evening. He still felt the chill from the loch. He'd helped Da and Kieran fish out Miss O'Callaghan's keys. It had been a literal needle in a haystack, but they'd found them. Thank providence that those damned keys hadn't floated away from Eilean Donan. Lachlan looked down the block and briefly wondered if he should make a mad dash to Reilly's pub for a bite. His first client of the day would be in around one and it was twelve-forty five, he likely only had about fifteen minutes if that, and since Da and Kieran were off work today, they would likely want a pint, and they wouldn't be taking "no" for an answer.

Lachlan sighed and entered the shop, and flipped the sign from closed to open. Lunch could wait until Aiden came in for his shift at two, which unfortunately was a full hour away. He might as well be taking lunch to work from now on to make sure this never happened again. Lachlan walked back to his office, and put his backpack on his desk, then walked over to the client cabinet where they stored all of their client's paperwork and drawings and unlocked it for the other artists.

The bell outside tinkled and Lachlan walked out to reception to greet the first guest of the day, and froze. Standing in front of him was Annalise O'Callaghan. She walked around his shop holding his album and biting her lower lip as she studied the photos and drawings that he knew were in there. Damn, she was sexy and beautiful.

"Can I help you, lass?" he asked her and smiled when Annalise looked at him and froze. "Annalise?"

Annalise shook her head and walked towards him and the desk.

"I want a tattoo," she said and handed him his album, pointing at a thistle and Celtic knot drawing. "How much is this one?"

"For you? Nothing," he told her. "Let's call it a first tattoo discount. Now what time should I book you for?" Lachlan clicked on the program they used to book appointments and looked at Annalise.

"Three good for you?" Lachlan asked. "It will only be a consultation, and you would be under no obligation to get that tattoo today until you like what you see."

Annalise nodded, and Lachlan penciled her in. "Alright Miss O'Callaghan you're ready to go, do you wish for me to explain what I will do?"

"No, my dad has tattoos, I don't need any explanations." Annalise smiled and looked around the shop, then back at him. "I should get going."

"Wait." Lachlan walked out from behind the desk. "How about we get dinner?"

Annalise smiled. "Do you ask all of your clients to dinner?"

"Just the beautiful ones." Lachlan smiled. "So how about

it? We can order in and we can talk. Meet at my house?" Annalise gave him a thin smile. "Or we can meet at yours."

"No, no, your house is magnificent. But we eat pizza, and I get to choose what toppings we get."

Lachlan laughed. "Fair enough."

An hour later, Lachlan met with Annalise at the front desk. The woman was standing beside Ivy, Skye Ink's secretary, and both women had their hands on their hips. Lachlan felt his good mood shift as he peered around the women to the other woman. She wore a low tank top showing her breasts and short shorts. She had tattoos all up and down her legs, and one that sat unfinished on her right arm. This was Tonya Banks, the woman who had broken his brother's heart over two years ago.

"She's here for you," Ivy growled, and Lachlan looked at her a dark eyebrow raised. Why him?

Lachlan stepped forward, "I am sorry Miss Banks, I am all booked for the day, maybe later in the month?" Tonya gave him her best smile, and squeezed her breasts together with her arms, trying to look the part of an innocent girl. *Hardly innocent, bitch.* Lachlan smiled back and turned to Ivy. "Schedule her for later in the month."

"Certainly." Ivy smiled as she backed away from Annalise to stand behind the reception counter. "Miss Banks, please come here so that I might schedule you for your appointment?"

Tonya brushed up against Lachlan, and the Scotsman shivered. From disgust or excitement? Annalise asked herself as she watched the woman walk to the desk. She was probably made of more plastic than actual woman. Annalise looked at Lachlan, who gently grabbed her arm and pulled her past reception. Annalise instantly regretted wanting a tattoo.

"So, I was thinking we could take a rain check on my tattoo," Annalise said as she followed him into his room. "I mean, if that's okay with you, I know you scheduled me for today, but honestly…"

"You're not ready for me to do the tattoo," Lachlan finished with a smirk. "It's alright lass, it's just a consultation after all."

"Of course, but how did you know I wasn't ready?"

"I have been a tattoo artist for ten years, when a client tells me they aren't ready it usually means they haven't thought it through."

"Oh." Annalise smiled and pushed a strand of hair from her face. "That makes sense."

Lachlan nodded and patted his artist chair. "Let's see what the tattoo will look like on you so you can make your decision."

"Alright," Annalise said as she sat down on the chair. "Will it hurt?"

"No, it's just a stencil." Lachlan told her as he put ointment on her arm. "Your tattoo will probably hurt depending on where you want it, I am doing this stencil on your arm where it's least likely to hurt, and easier for you to see."

"What parts of the body would it hurt to get a tattoo?"

"The ankle, foot, ribs, neck, and hands. At least that's what clients have told me. I only have tattoos on my arm, and shoulder. So I cannot tell you much about pain." He smiled. "It's also a matter of how the person tolerates pain as well. Women can usually tolerate pain better than men, but again it depends on the person."

Lachlan smoothed the paper down on her arm and pressed firmly. He put more ointment on the paper to wet it and then let it sit for a few seconds before peeling it off carefully.

"Here, see if that's what you wanted." Lachlan handed her a small mirror.

Annalise looked at her arm in the mirror and smiled. The Celtic knot was beautiful and complemented the Thistle well.

"It's exquisite."

He looked at her, his eyes dark. "Not as beautiful as the woman who will wear it."

Annalise felt her face warm as she looked at the tattoo. Anything to keep from acknowledging Lachlan's flirting. He was handsome, she had to admit but she wasn't yet ready to date. It was one thing to visit with him and share pizza and maybe a movie. Dating was out of the cards, everything that had happened in the relationship with Joseph had caused more than second guessing and what Annalise called her cowardly lion phase. She was too afraid to travel down the yellow brick road to Oz and request the wonderful wizard to give her what Joseph took from her.

Lachlan stared at Annalise, she was distant now and he instantly regretted saying anything to her. If she didn't want to see him again, he would understand, but he wouldn't let her go without a fight. Annalise had something about her that Lachlan couldn't place, and it drew him in like a moth to a flame.

"I should go," Annalise told him, turning to look at him. "It's a beautiful tattoo. Thank you." She kissed him on his cheek. "I will see you tonight and let you know my decision when I have one."

CHAPTER SEVEN

Annalise climbed out of the shower and quickly dressed. She was due at Lachlan's in almost an hour, and so far everything wasn't going as planned. She got an email from her boss in Seattle; he begged her to take back her job from the overly enthusiastic recent university graduate.

She promptly, and politely told him no, ignoring the sudden panic that welled up inside her when she remembered she would soon have to look for employment. She still had her father helping her with money, but she soon hoped to change that. Hoping to walk on her own two feet once again. Annalise brushed her hair, put it up into a messy bun, and ran naked into her room to dress. She had chosen a black cocktail dress that stopped at her knees. The neckline was low to show the tops of her breasts, but not too revealing if she and Lachlan wanted a night on the town.

Finally dressed, Annalise walked out of the house. She climbed into her car and prepared to leave when a stark white hand grabbed her door, the beautiful pale face of a woman appearing. Her hair was short and black, tied in a crimson ribbon which matched her lips.

"Can I help you ma'am?" Annalise asked her and the woman smiled.

"Why yes, you can Miss O'Callaghan," she answered. Annalise, for a reason she didn't understand, felt cold dread fill the pit of her stomach.

Lachlan looked up at the clock. Almost ten, and no sign of Annalise. He was worrying she would never show up. He kept himself busy and tried not to think about it.

"She will be here," Kieran told him when he caught Lachlan looking at the clock. "Call her if you have to."

"I don't want to seem like I am pushing her, it is her choice if she wishes to show up or not." Lachlan wiped his client's arm and finished the tattoo. "Better to be the man who doesn't push, than the man who does and loses the girl."

Kieran looked at him. "Aye, but then you could be the man who didn't care."

Lachlan snorted. "Wise words coming from a self-proclaimed ladies' man."

Kieran chuckled. "Asshole."

Lachlan patted his client's arm and walked him to Ivy so she could ring him up.

"Hear anything?" Ivy asked him when the client left.

"No, not yet," he told her. "I fear she won't ever show."

"Now you're being a pessimist," Ivy said, giving him a look of displeasure. "She will show. Have a little faith."

"What are you looking for?" Annalise asked, eyeing her car door and the lock button.

The woman followed her gaze and smiled. Her teeth, a bright white harshly contrasting with her blood-red lips.

"Not what, who am I looking for more like," she said in an unknown thick accent that was unrecognizable.

"Then who are you looking for?"

The woman bent over until her nose was close to Annalise's own nose. Annalise moved away, uncomfortable.

"A woman," the woman told her amused at having made Annalise uncomfortable. "Her name is Illona. She came this way, even lived near here, and I thought perhaps you would know of her."

Annalise looked away from her, her heart skipping a beat.

"Well?" the woman asked sweetly, and Annalise looked at her.

"I don't know her, maybe you should ask the neighbor down the road. She's older and knows more about the area than I do," Annalise said unsure about what to say or do.

"Pity, I am sorry to have bothered you miss O'Callaghan." The woman shut her door and walked away without another word. Annalise felt the dread leave her; stupid to feel such a silly thing the woman had only been looking for this Illona. Maybe they were sisters or something?

Annalise sighed, and even though she knew she shouldn't, she lowered her window and called out to her.

"What's your name?"

The woman stopped walking and turned to her. "Snow, Miss O'Callaghan."

Snow disappeared into the darkness before Annalise could ask her the one question her brain screamed at her not to ask. "Is there some way I can help you find her?"

Annalise rolled the window up and shivered. She could have sworn she heard a female voice whispering, "Yes, Miss O'Callaghan."

Snow

I watched as she drove away in that silly horseless carriage. Humans are so fickle, stupid, and blind to see what they do to themselves. Stupid enough to stare death straight in her face, and not even flinch. This girl, Annalise O'Callaghan, is a willing target, naïve and as ignorant as the rest. But, she saw through Pilanin's disguise, not everyone can, which makes this young woman special. Now if only I knew why she was so special, then I could decide what I was going to do with her. She'd lied about Illona. It was in her eyes, and body language. How does she know her? Who knows, but the stupid human has just given me my invitation into her life, and will next invite me into her home. Big mistake.

Skye Ink
Kyleakin, Scotland

11:30 P.M.

It was 11:30 when Annalise pulled into the back lot behind Skye Ink and went inside. She hoped to find Lachlan waiting for her, but found his brother, Kieran behind the reception counter counting money. He looked up at her when she entered.

"So you came after all," he said with a smile that brightened his handsome face. "Good thing too, go through the back and up the stairs. Lachlan should be upstairs."

Annalise passed him and into the back of the shop where the artists work. She followed the hallway to the back door. She found the staircase Kieran told her about and climbed them. The door at the top was wide open as if letting someone know they were welcome to come in. The windows were open and the curtains, an almost silk material, blew in the soft cool spring breeze.

"Hello," Annalise called out, knocking on the door.

"Make yourself comfortable lass, I will be just a moment," Lachlan called from somewhere in the apartment.

Annalise walked in. It was not what she expected; the room was large with a sectional couch, and a flat screen television on the wall, a few feet from the TV sat a small table with a lamp. On that table lay a book. It was open so that the book's front and back cover was face up. Annalise picked it up, and she felt excitement when she stared at her book. Lachlan had been reading it!

"I bought that the week we met," Lachlan said when he entered the living room.

Annalise smiled at him, he looked so handsome and sexy standing in front of her. He wore a button-up shirt which showed off his muscles when he moved. He smelled like man and his Axe brand body wash.

"Are you enjoying it?" Annalise asked, trying to ignore the heat building between her thighs.

"Aye, very intense and very imaginative," Lachlan told her with a wide smile. "Been reading it repeatedly, been waiting to read the second book. Unfortunately, I haven't had the time to get the second from the bookstore." He walked over to her, replaced the book on the table, and brushed a stray hair from her face.

"You look beautiful, lass."

Annalise smiled and turned away, her cheeks warm. "You're just saying that, I am not that beautiful. I am sure there are other women you have been with who were better than me."

Lachlan frowned. "I meant all I said, lass."

"I am sorry, I didn't mean it like that, just that..."

"Just what lass, too afraid to take a compliment and see the beauty within, and out?"

"No," Annalise said, averting her gaze.

"So, Pizza?" Lachlan asked quickly, changing the subject, and Annalise gratefully nodded her head, her stomach growling.

An hour later, they sat next to each other watching the new Channing Tatum movie, and nursing a glass of red wine. So far, the night was going great, and Lachlan hadn't brought up why she was so self-conscious about herself when she was complimented. She hoped it stayed that way. She really wanted a friend, needed a friend.

"Channing Tatum is so sexy," Annalise commented.

"Oh my god, you know it, girl," Lachlan said in his best mock girl voice, his Scottish accent harshly contrasting with it, and causing her to laugh until her sides were sore. She laid her head in his lap and curled up, and then it happened. A great big fart burst out of her just as Lachlan bent over to tickle her and make her laugh harder.

Annalise's face warmed, and Lachlan laughed harder than she was, and fell halfway on top of her. Annalise laughed again because his laughter was contagious, but still felt so embarrassed about the fart.

"I am so, so sorry Lachlan," she said when they got a breather, but Lachlan shook his head. They only broke into a fit of giggles once more.

Lachlan grabbed her shoulder, and turned her to face him, and pressed his lips to hers. Their laughter silenced for the moment. Annalise moaned and wrapped her arms around his neck and pressed against him. He tasted like the red wine they shared, and spice. Lachlan's hands slid down from her shoulders to cup her ass and pulled her onto his lap. Lachlan slid his hands up her body and pulled the top of her dress down and pulled one of her breasts into his mouth.

Annalise moaned, and unbuttoned his shirt, and pushed it aside to reveal tan skin, and muscles, and the front part of his Celtic knot tattoo. Lachlan shrugged off his shirt. Annalise slid her hands up and down his chest and down further to the waistband of his jeans and unbuttoned them, sliding her hand into his jeans and under his boxers.

"Good God, lass," Lachlan moaned when she found his cock.

Lachlan pulled her into another kiss and pulled her dress down to her waist, freeing her breasts. Lachlan took one breast into his mouth and suckled.

Annalise moaned, arching her back, allowing him better access. Lachlan flicked his tongue around her nipple, lifted himself up with her still on his lap, and removed his jeans and boxers. Annalise looked at Lachlan fully naked before her, biting her lower lip. Excitement and lust flashed in her eyes. Lachlan didn't think he could get any harder.

Lachlan lifted her dress to her waist, and slid her panties off, his cock pressed at her warm and moist center. He kissed her deeply, and pumped his hips, the tip of his cock barely entering her. Annalise moaned and lowered herself on it, letting him slide in further. Lachlan broke the kiss and looked her in the eye.

"Be sure," he hissed, flexing his hips entering her just a little, and then pulling out.

Annalise whimpered.

"Please," she begged. "I want you."

Lachlan groaned, and in one swift thrust of his hips, entered her. Annalise moaned, falling forward onto his chest.

"Go on fairy, take what you want," he said, and Annalise moved.

She threw back her head and moaned. Lachlan squeezed her breasts, and slid his hands down her stomach and to her clit, rubbing it with his thumb. Annalise felt the orgasm build, and threw back her head once more before falling into sweet, sweet bliss. Lachlan pulled her head down and kissed her passionately. He broke the kiss to grab her hips and guide her up and down his cock until she came again, and again. Lachlan moaned as she squeezed his cock, his own orgasm building. With one last deep thrust, Lachlan spilled himself deep within her, Annalise followed behind him, milking him until he had no more to give.

Annalise fell on top of his chest, breathing hard.

"Oh, my God," Annalise said, and Lachlan laughed.

"Was it that good you have to curse God?" Lachlan asked. Annalise looked at him and gave him a sated smile.

"Yes, God probably hath never felt such a good feeling," Annalise told him, and Lachlan laughed once more.

The couple lay there, in the quiet for a few moments. Lachlan rubbed his fingertips up and down her back, finally breaking the silence to ask what Annalise hoped he wouldn't ask.

"Who abused you?"

"Lachlan, please leave it alone. It's in the past."

"Annalise, I only want to know who caused you so much pain."

Annalise sighed and climbed off him to sit on the couch.

CHAPTER EIGHT

What had she been thinking? Having sex with a man she barely knew. She found her panties and pulled them on and turned to Lachlan. A grim look was set on his face. He looked her up and down, then found his own jeans and pulled them on. He looked at her once more.

"Is everything alright lass?" he asked her as he pulled on his shirt.

"Fine. Everything is fine," Annalise said looking anywhere but him.

Lachlan didn't believe a word of it. He had fucked up— he knew regret when he saw it. He ran a hand through his hair and pulled it back with a band.

"Would you like me to get you anything?"

Annalise eyed the door, which they had forgotten when they had their moment of intense passion, then looked at him.

"No, I am fine," *No, you're not!* "I need to go, I have work." *Liar!*

"Alright, I will see you soon." He smiled at her. "I will see you again, right?"

"Yeah, of course." *Liar!* Annalise winced as her mind screamed at her. She turned and almost ran out the open door. "I will call you later tonight, maybe tomorrow."

Lachlan nodded and watched her leave. He cursed and sat down and let his head hang.

"I am so sorry, lass," he whispered. "I am such a fucking idiot."

Annalise shuffled into her house, threw her purse onto the couch and walked to her bedroom. She threw herself onto her bed and buried her face into her pillow. Hot tears streamed down her cheeks, dampening the pillow. *Why are you so fucked up, couldn't you have just accepted what happened?*

"Damn you Joseph!" Annalise screamed, punching her pillow, her tears coming hard and fast. "Damn you."

Annalise cried until she fell asleep. It was late in the afternoon when she woke next the day, her cell phone ringing in her purse. She shuffled into the living room, still emotionally exhausted, and to her purse, fumbling around inside until she found her cell phone. Annalise frowned at the caller id, unknown.

"Hello?" she answered.

"Hello, Annalise," a familiar male voice answered back, and she froze.

"Brendan?" she asked, a smile finding its way on her face.

"Yes, how are you doing cuz?" he laughed.

"Great, how is the military treating you?"

"Treating me well, they have let me go on permanent leave."

"When?" Annalise walked into the kitchen. She grabbed a glass from the cupboard as well as the orange juice from the refrigerator, and poured herself a glass.

"Almost three weeks ago. Uncle James sent me a ticket to Scotland this week too."

"For a holiday?"

"No, permanently." Annalise frowned she could hear the strain in her cousin's voice. They'd grown up together, and she had heard no sadness or frustration coming from him. He was always positive, and very hyper. Had the military drowned that part of him?

"Why?" She heard him sigh.

"Grandma and Grandpa cut out my inheritance. You know as well as I do, they hadn't liked my mom, and despite that dislike of her, my choice to join the military." He sighed once more to cover up the pain she heard in his voice. "Mom and Dad passed almost three months ago, I guess James told you?

Annalise felt as if her heart leapt into her throat. Aunt Michelle and Uncle Misha were dead? "How... How did they die?"

"They were both found in their home, Mom in the living room, and Dad in his office." Brendan swallowed. "They were both shot execution style."

Annalise covered her mouth and tried not to cry out. Why them? Why did they have to die? Who could they have possibly hurt? Misha and Michelle had been positive souls, and very generous. Maybe a little trusting, but they hadn't deserved to die so horribly. She prayed they had felt little pain.

"When will you be coming to Scotland?" Annalise whispered, afraid that her voice would break.

"I should be in today. I'm supposed to call James when I land."

"Don't bother, just give me what airport you will be at, and I will pick you up. You can stay in my spare bedroom. I will call Dad on the way." Brendan gave her his landing time and the airport name.

"Thanks Annalise, I will see you soon."

"You're welcome." He hung up, and Annalise dialed her father, sobbing when he answered.

"Annalise, are you okay, love? Talk to me." His soothing Irish voice came through the phone.

"Why didn't you tell me they were dead?"

"Who, Annalise?"

"Aunt Michelle, and Uncle Misha."

James sighed. "Brendan called, didn't he?"

"Yes," she choked out. "Why didn't you tell me?"

"You had a lot to deal with, and I didn't want to cause you anymore grief. After what happened between you and Joseph, you were a complete mess, and I still didn't know if you've bounced back."

At the mention of Joseph, Annalise winced. She hadn't completely gone back to normal and having sex with Lachlan didn't help matters. She understood her father wanted to protect her. But it was wrong to keep the deaths of family from family, especially from her, his daughter. True, she and James never got to have those moments that only a father and daughter could have while she was growing up, but it didn't give him the right to keep it from her, no matter her past or how gruesome it was.

"Sweet, you there?" James asked, worry lacing his thick Irish accent. "Annalise, please talk to me, darling."

Annalise shook her head to clear her thoughts. "Sorry Dad, I'm fine, just a little upset." *Not just about Aunt Michelle and Uncle Misha, but about Lachlan too. God, I was a fool for being so weak.*

James sighed. "I know I should have told you, but their deaths were a low blow. Your cousin needed help, and so too does the child my brother, your uncle Misha, left behind."

"Child, what child?" The very thought of her uncle being unfaithful to her aunt made everything grind to a halt.

"His name is Brody, and he had been born to an American woman. He is ten, he was living with Misha, and Michelle, and was at school at the time of their deaths."

"Poor kid, where will he go? Does Brendan know?" Another woman! Just who was this woman Uncle Misha had felt inclined to cheat on his wife with?

"Brendan knows, and he will take Brody in. The kid's mom was found unfit to take him, and he has no other relatives." *That you know of.*

"Have the authorities found out who killed Misha and Michelle?"

"Nothing yet, when I know you'll know." Annalise closed her eyes and clenched her jaw in annoyance. She hated when he told her that. It had been the same saying when Badb had died. *He still hasn't even told me that.*

"Okay," she whispered, not willing to bring on a fight along with the bad news.

"I'm going to let you go now, unless there is something more you wish to share with me?" *Yes!*

"No." Annalise squeezed her eyes shut as more tears flowed. "I love you, Dad."

"I love you too, darling." James hung up, and Annalise laid her head on the cool kitchen counter.

Annalise wiped her tears and grabbed her car keys, leaving in a hazy fog. The world seemed very slow at that moment. Almost as if the world refused to move beneath her. She climbed into her car, and pulled out of the driveway, and onto the A87 headed to the one place she knew.

Skye Ink

Kyleakin, Scotland

Lachlan stared down at his mother's arm as he touched up the small Celtic knot she had gotten when Dad and she had first married. This time though, he was closing the arch, and making it a complete ring, with rose embellishments, and a Celtic princess and her knight on horseback in the likeness of his mom and dad. He wiped the blood, plasma, and extra color from her arm and finished the last bit of the Celtic circle. He had just shaded it when the bell above the shop's door tinkled and he heard Ivy cry out.

He and his mother looked at each other concerned. Lachlan stepped off his peddle and set his tattoo machine down on the counter. After wiping his mom's arm, he pulled off his gloves. He stood and walked out of his station, his mom following close behind. Lachlan broke into a jog when he saw Annalise kneeling on the floor in Ivy's arms, her loud sobs filling the shop, her body shaking. He knelt down next to her, gathering her from Ivy's arms and into his own, cradling her against his chest.

"What's wrong, lass?" Lachlan asked rubbing her back as she sobbed. "Please lass, tell me."

His mother knelt down in front of them. "Let's get her into the apartment before any other client's come in." She helped him stand. Lachlan put his arm under Annalise's knees and carried her to the back and upstairs to his apartment.

He sat down on his couch with her in his lap, rubbing her back and whispering reassuring words in her ear as he rocked her. Something had happened to the lass, and he hoped it wasn't their one-night stand. If it was the reason she was crying so hard, he was an even bigger idiot for that. And a prick. He wasn't Kieran; he was more sensitive to his woman's needs. Lachlan's heart skipped a beat. His woman? When had she become his?

His mother came into the living room with a mug and sat next to him. "Here sweetheart, some hot tea. It's chamomile, it will soothe you."

Annalise took the mug and took a sip. "Thank you."

Cassie smiled. "No problem, now why don't you tell us what happened."

Annalise rubbed her eyes, looked up at Lachlan, and scooted off his lap onto the couch next to his mother. Lachlan felt his heart lurch at the sight. He was a dick.

"My aunt, and uncle were found dead three months ago," Annalise told them. "Both in the head." Her lower lip trembled, and she let out a sob. Cassie rubbed her back, her face solemn.

"We are sorry for your loss."

Lachlan felt happier that it wasn't him, but truly felt sadness for her loss. She'd been very close to them, and she was suffering. He should sweep in and do something, but he didn't know what. He'd never really dealt with a death in the family. His grandparents on his father's side died when he had been an infant, and his father was an only child. He never met his mother's family.

"Where were you headed, dear?" Cassie asked.

"To Inverness airport to pick up my cousin," Annalise answered. She took another sip of tea, the chamomile strong, and her mind feeling wonderfully muddled. "He is supposed to be landing soon, and he is moving in with me. I am supposed to be there. I have to be there. I have to go." She stood but fell back, Cassie and Lachlan caught her.

"That's two hours away, and you are in no shape to be going anywhere," Cassie told her. She looked at her son. "Get your brother and pick up her cousin."

Lachlan nodded and looked at Annalise standing. "What is his name?"

"Brendan," Annalise told him before she slumped over into his mother's lap, out cold.

Lachlan reached for her, but his mother slapped his hands away. "She's fine, I put a bit of sleeping med in the tea, the kind I give your father when he cannot sleep. It isn't dangerous, so don't worry. Go get her cousin."

CHAPTER NINE

"Wonder who killed her aunt, and uncle." Kieran wondered for the fifteenth time as they sat waiting for Annalise's cousin, Brendan to come in from his flight.

"I don't know Kieran. She didn't say, and mum wouldn't let her, anyway. She was too upset." Lachlan handed Kieran the name card they made. "Your turn." He crossed his arms and watched. They didn't even know what this guy looked like, just a name.

"That him?" Kieran asked thirty minutes later.

He and Lachlan watched a man wearing a camouflage suit walk towards them. His black hair was shaved at the sides and with longer hair styled to sit atop his head to give him a head banger rock star look. His handsomely tanned face was covered in a five o'clock shadow, and he didn't look pleased to see them.

"I'm Brendan."

The two highlanders stood.

"I'm Lachlan, this is my brother Kieran. Annalise sent us."

"What's happened to her?"

"We will explain on the way," Kieran told him as he and Lachlan walked him to the car.

Brendan broke into a smile. "A Charger, holy shit." He palmed the sides and walked around the car. "First time, I saw one of these beauties was in the Dukes of Hazard." He looked at the brothers. "You Dukes fans?"

Kieran rolled his eyes. "Oh aye, Lachlan is huge, he has a fancy for the girl." He climbed into the car. "Don't get him started."

Lachlan opened the trunk. "Mine isn't authentic, and yes I am a fan."

"It's a Charger dude, doesn't have to be the same color. Besides, I like your ride. The black color with the white wolves running on the sides onto the hood is awesome."

Lachlan chuckled and handed him the keys. "You want to drive it?"

Brendan laughed, threw his baggage into the trunk, and grabbed the keys. "Shit, yeah!"

Annalise woke to the handsome face of her cousin, Brendan. He was fast asleep in a chair beside her bed, the worry lines clear across his face as he slept. She sat up and stretched before silently climbing out of the bed. She covered him up with the blanket from her bed and walked out of the room. When she found the living room was empty, she looked in Lachlan's bedroom and nearly jumped out of her skin. The Scotsman lay on the bed on his stomach passed out; the blankets kicked to the floor, and the sheets pooling around him partially covering his bottom half. Annalise looked back out into the living room and then crept into the room and Lachlan. *Just a peek, that's all.* She lifted the sheet slowly, watching Lachlan as he slept. She lifted it higher and bit her lip as she stared down at his naked ass and bared back. He was tanned here too, and his ass was well formed. Annalise knew he would look sexy in a pair of tight leather pants, or jeans. She suddenly wanted to see the rest of him, just to refresh that memory of the one-night stand they'd had.

Annalise lowered the sheet and closed his door and walked back to the bed. She climbed onto it, and slowly crept up to Lachlan. When she was close to his left shoulder Annalise shoved him softly. He was heavier than he looked; she gave him one last shove and Lachlan turned over in his sleep taking her with him, trapping her hand beneath his left shoulder, and causing her to have to climb on top of him. Annalise shook her head. *Great, just great Anna, you have totally messed this one up. If he wakes up, he will expect something from you.*

Lachlan moaned in his sleep, and flexed his hips, and Annalise froze when she felt his erection brush the inseam of her jeans through the sheet. He was evidently having a glorious dream, and Annalise suspected it might have to do with her. She pulled her arm, finally getting out from behind his shoulder. She turned to climb off of him when she felt a set of powerful hands grasp her hips, keeping her rooted to her spot.

"Fuck!" Annalise said, closing her eyes.

"If it is what you want, I am only happy to help you. However, you're wearing far too many clothes, and that, lass, is disappointing." Lachlan said, his voice laced with sleep. He arranged himself, and groaned, wanting to push himself inside her but knowing that if he tried anything, he most likely would be labeled as a rapist, and get his ass kicked by Brendan in the next room.

Annalise looked down at him and gave him a sheepish smile. "I... Erm... I was just trying to cover you up, you looked cold."

Lachlan chuckled. "Or you were trying to look at me. I know what you were doing lass."

Annalise scoffed. "You do not, if you did you would have

woken up while I was looking at you earlier." She clapped her hand over her mouth, and Lachlan laughed.

"Told you I knew what you were doing, and lass, if you wanted a peek, you could have asked. It's not like we are hiding from each other, right?" Lachlan said, and Annalise's face warmed.

"You are an ass." She finally said as she climbed off of him and stomped to the door. "And just so you know, I am hiding from you. If I had not been so upset yesterday, I would never have come back here to you." Annalise turned on her heel and left the room.

Lachlan jumped up, wrapped the sheet around his middle, and ran after her.

"Annalise, I am sorry, please don't go," he called to her, running into the living room just as she slammed the front door. Lachlan opened it, and stood on the top of his stair, watching as she ran to her car and peeled away. He spun on his heel and punched the door frame. Lachlan looked up to find his mother standing beside Brendan.

Brendan looked him up and down while his mother shook her head with a small frown.

"Now don't start," Lachlan began, but Cassie raised her hand.

"No, don't you start son, she was already emotionally unstable, and what did you do? Acted like a freaking Neanderthal in heat!" Cassie scolded, grabbing her keys from her pocket and turned to Brendan. "Brendan, I can take you to the house and drop you off if you would like."

Brendan shook his head. "I would rather stay with Lachlan. I know my cousin. She will be like El Nino blowing through Florida, and I do not want to get caught up in that storm. Besides, I need a job, and Lachlan and Kieran offered me a spot at Skye Ink."

Cassie nodded, gave her son a disappointed look, and left

the apartment.

"Fucking bastard!" Annalise screamed, slamming her house door behind her. She threw off her shoes, and walked into her living, and screamed when she was met at the door by her father.

"Am I missing something?" he asked as she pushed past him to stomp into the kitchen, and grabbed a coke from the refrigerator.

"Only the biggest Scottish asshole in the world."

James raised an eyebrow. "And this asshole would be?"

Annalise popped her coke's tab and took a long drink.

"One Lachlan Macleod, womanizer, and biggest asshole in the world."

"Hm." Was all her father said.

Annalise stared at him, and her stomach leapt into her throat. "You know him, don't you?"

James nodded. "Murdoch's son, one of my childhood friends. Last time I saw Murdoch, all three of his children were home. Lachlan didn't seem the womanizing type, and I don't quite agree with the asshole part darling, unless you count his brother Kieran, that boy is a known womanizer, and can be quite an asshole."

"Not the Lachlan I know, he would rather wine and dine a girl then sleep with her to get what he wants."

James clenched one of his fists. "Did he wine, and dine you, and sleep with you?"

"An honest mistake, and now he won't let it go, when all I want to do is forget it happened."

"Indeed." James frowned. "Unfortunately, my darling, it takes two grown adults to tango."

"What!?" Annalise said "But he..."

"Did you go to bed with him, consensually?" James rubbed his chin.

"Well yeah, of course," Annalise said. "But that's not the

point."

"Well darling, what is the point?"

Annalise opened and closed her mouth. What was the point? Why was she so angry with Lachlan? They had done something normal even, so why the anger? Lachlan wasn't Joseph, he was kinder, had been gentler when they had made love. Despite having joked with her that afternoon, he wasn't an ass, nor was he pompous, or bad tempered as Joseph was. In fact, Lachlan had made light of her having been caught trying to see him naked once more. He wasn't Joseph, she realized, this was why she was angry, she wanted revenge against her ex, and Lachlan was not Joseph, and that made her upset, she wanted him to be. This was bad, very bad, Joseph should be out of sight, and out of mind, and yet he reared his devilishly handsome, sneering face back into her life. When would he be gone? When would she be free?

Maybe Lachlan thought he was her way to freedom? That angered her more than Lachlan not being Joseph. She should be able to do this on her own, no help needed from a man.

"I think I may have overreacted Daddy. What should I do?"

James walked to the refrigerator and grabbed a bottle of water. "I guess you're just going to apologize somehow."

"How?" Annalise rubbed her face. "It's embarrassing."

James sat down at the kitchen table. "I know my darling, but that's something you will need to deal with." He took a drink. "Forget Joseph, live your life, and let Lachlan know you and him are alright. You and him shared one night, and likely he's feeling like an ass, while you are feeling angry." He smiled. "Maybe, I am only saying maybe, something will come out of your time with Lachlan."

Annalise smiled. Yeah maybe it could be all she ever wanted, or maybe it could become worse than what she'd had with Joseph.

CHAPTER TEN

Brendan steadied the tattoo machine above the grapefruit and pressed gently into it, making a thin line with the ink and needle. Beside him, his mentor Aiden grunted his satisfaction. The man was talkative when he wanted to be, but he had become quieter now that he'd begun mentoring Brendan, testing him non-stop for the tattooing license he was supposed to receive so he could be a full-time tattoo artist.

Lachlan walked over and looked down at the grapefruit.

"I think we can safely move you onto pig skin, lad." He looked at Aiden, seeking consultation.

"I think he's ready to jump into tattooing, he has the experience. He is just holding back," Aiden commented, and Lachlan stared down at Brendan.

Brendan slid his foot from the peddle and put down the tattoo machine. He looked at both men and gave an uncomfortable smile. "It was a long time ago." He rolled up his right sleeve and showed them the Celtic stag. "My mom and dad encouraged me to be a tattoo artist. My friend Joshua owned a shop with his father. We were close to working full time when he and his dad went missing. The shop got a new manager, and I went into the military."

Lachlan clapped him on his shoulder. "Doesn't matter how long it's been, lad, you never really lose the knowledge you earn. Aiden believes you're ready, and I trust him, and you." He looked around the shop and gave a wide excited grin when his sister, Riley walked in. "And I have your first client, come meet her."

Brendan stood and followed Lachlan until they stopped in front of a tall and skinny young woman with long incredibly curly red hair, a lip stud, and red lips. Her eyes were dark green while her creamy, freckled skin was free of blemishes. She smiled at Lachlan, flicked her hands in the air, and jumped into his arms.

"I missed you Lachlan," the woman said as her hands moved in front of her when Lachlan had pushed her back at arm's length. "Where's Kieran?"

"He is out with Lillian, " Lachlan signed. "But never mind that, I have a new artist I want you to try out. He's an apprentice but has tattooed before."

Riley signed back. "You want me to be his guinea pig?"

"Yes, you're a woman, and that would keep him from fucking up your pretty skin," Lachlan laughed.

Riley rolled her eyes. "Asshole." She signed, looked around, and then pointed at Brendan who froze. "He the new meat?"

Lachlan made his fist nod. Riley walked up to Brendan and looked him up and down. Brendan felt shivers going down his spine.

"Alright, he can tattoo me," she said using her voice, which was louder than it should be. "But I choose what." Brendan nodded quickly. Riley grabbed his arm and walked him to the back rooms.

Lachlan chuckled and looked at Aiden who raised one

dark brow and grunted before walking off to get his next client. The bell over the shop rang, and Lachlan turned, smiling at Annalise. She walked into the shop clutching a large stack of papers and a large canvas bag. She gave him a sheepish smile when she caught him looking at her.

"What are you up to, lassie?" he asked, his voice husky.

"Putting up an editorial ad for a job, hopefully someone will see it and call me to edit their books or papers," Annalise said handing him the stack of papers so she could hang up one of the ad's on Skye Ink's cork board.

"Or you could work here," Lachlan blurted out, and Annalise fumbled with the ad as she looked at him, a little startled.

"Oh no, no, no," she refused. "Not going to happen. We have terrible history Lachlan, well not unpleasant history, just an incident between us that should never have happened." Annalise bit her lip. "It would be strange, wouldn't it?"

Lachlan sighed and rubbed his unshaven face before placing his hands on her thin shoulders. "Think about this lass, you're looking for work, I have an opening. We did something you regret, and yet you still come to Skye Ink to put up your ad, and hold a semi-decent conversation without blowing your beautiful little head off on me, and you think working here would be strange." He chuckled. "It should be me who should be worried about working with you, what with the pent-up rage you have in that wee body of yours."

Annalise smiled shyly. "I will think about it." She turned back to the corkboard and pinned the ad, then hefted her stack of ads and walked to the door.

"Annalise," Lachlan called, and she turned and looked at him. "In case you wanted to know, I don't regret the time we spent with one another, even if it was only for the night."

Annalise blushed and rushed out of Skye Ink and her car.

Lachlan turned and walked into the back towards his office, Aiden waited by the door.

"How is Brendan getting along with Riley?"

"He is nearly done with the rose on her shoulder blade," Aiden said, and Lachlan nodded.

"Come get me when he finishes, I would like to see how well he did with it and see how my sister feels about him being our newest artist."

Aiden nodded, and Lachlan walked into his office and sat at the desk. His phone buzzed, and he dug it out of his pocket, and smiled.

I will take the job. But I have conditions. Will come back tomorrow afternoon

Annalise

An hour later Riley and Brendan came into the office, Aiden behind them, his arms crossed.

"Let's see your work aye?" Lachlan asked gently peeling the bandage from the very realistic rose and colorful hummingbird. He looked at Brendan and gave him a nod of approval. "Very well done, but let's see what my little sister thinks."

Brendan's eyes widened. Sister! He swallowed uncomfortably. Riley looked at him, and smiled, her green eyes sparkling.

"He's your new artist, and I recommend him." She winked at him. "Make sure he stays, I like him." With that said Riley left the shop, bopping Ivy on her head, and waving at a young teenager who sat watching her mother getting a tattoo on her way out.

"Well, congratulations, lad. Welcome to Skye Ink," Lachlan said. "I will help you get your license, and Aiden here will clean up one room for you. Equipment is provided the first time by Skye Ink for new hires." Aiden left the room, and Lachlan opened his filing cabinet and handed him a packet. "All you need to know about us is in the packet, and you must sign the forms in the back." He smiled. "Welcome to Skye Ink once more."

Brendan looked down at the packet, his heart racing, his dream job finally in his grasp. If only Mom and Dad were here. He swallowed, and all the money he was going to be making here would go to a home, and a kid brother he barely even knew.

"Do you need anything else, Brendan?" Lachlan asked when the other man just stood there in front of him.

Brendan shook his head and walked out of the office as if in a dream, and in that dream had been Riley Macleod, a beautiful deaf woman, and the first person who had given him his first shot in years. He rubbed his right ear where no sound would ever be heard in it again, and wondered if a kid brother would mind, and if maybe he should ask Riley to teach him sign language.

CHAPTER ELEVEN

What had she been thinking, taking a job with Lachlan at Skye Ink? Annalise groaned and climbed out of bed and shuffled into the kitchen for a coffee. She could refuse, back out, and what? Run away because they shared a night with one another? She felt cowardly, not the headstrong woman she knew she was. Even her father agreed she had let that one night get to her. Lachlan wasn't a bad man, he was just not bad enough for her. How bad does he have to be? Joseph Declan bad? Her mind screamed at her, and she screamed back her agreement and winced. She'd hated her life with Joseph, and she feared him. Lachlan would never do the things Joseph had done to her, and why should she want him too!

Annalise cleaned out her cup and dressed. She needed help, she decided, professional help. She was fucked up in the head for even wanting a man as abusive as Joseph had been. Instead of saying Lachlan was bad for her, she should say she was bad for Lachlan. Annalise sat down at her computer, and started the browser, and typed psychiatric help, and found a listing on Skye not too far from Skye Ink.

She set up her appointment to go before her first day at the parlor.

Annalise found the office two blocks from Skye Ink and went inside. She instantly regretted choosing the place when she saw Lachlan Macleod sitting on one couch, reading a tattooing magazine. He looked up, and smirked when she walked in, and scooted over to give her a spot on the couch. Annalise looked around the crowded room and had no choice but to sit next to him.

"Small Scotland, aye?" He told her with a chuckle

"Yeah," was all she said.

An hour passed when finally an older man, Annalise assumed, was the psychiatrist called for the both of them to come on back. The couple followed him, confused, until they were in his office with the door closed.

"You're probably wondering why I called both of you in, eh?" he said to them, pulling their files and laying them on his desk. "Law states I cannot tell other people what's in another's file, but I am old, and I see that you both are quite close, although one of you is less likely to admit. But, I also promised a beautiful woman, a colleague of mine at St. Andrews, that I would counsel both of you simultaneously."

Lachlan groaned and rubbed his face. "Mum," he muttered.

Annalise closed her eyes. Only one woman she knew, and that was Cassie. How dare she butt into her personal life!

"Now we are going to start, Annalise, why don't you go first."

"About what?" She bit out. "I should turn you in, not tell you my problems."

The older man inclined his head. "You may indeed, I am retiring soon anyway. You can't touch me, now talk."

"Fine, you want me to start, then here is something for you!" Annalise snapped.

She told him about Lachlan, their one-night stand, and how she viewed him. She even told him how angry she still was at Lachlan, and she didn't know why. Lachlan stared at her, his dark eyebrows raised, and jaw tight with frustration, his forest green eyes alight with pain.

"So now I work with him, and I can't take back what we did!"

The older man nodded and looked at Lachlan. "How do you feel about this?"

"Ashamed, angry I let her down, upset I hurt her." Lachlan looked at Annalise. "If I could take it back I would lass. I am so sorry."

Annalise saw the pain on his face and could swear she felt his shame. He's hid it so well, so well you were an idiot for not seeing he was sorry for what he's done.

"How does that make you feel Annalise?"

Annalise fidgeted. "I don't want, or need, your apology. It's not your fault, it's mine. I guess I got too carried away with my past." She looked back at the psychiatrist. "Which is why I wanted to talk to you."

"Ah yes, about Joseph." Mr. Schmitz looked at Lachlan, who stood and went to leave when Mr. Schmitz said. "It's often better to talk with those who have been through violence rather than with someone who hasn't. I have a degree miss O'Callaghan, but Mr. Macleod has experience, and that may be what you need right now."

"I am paying you, a psychiatrist."

Mr. Schmitz raised his hand, silencing her protest. "No charge, I can no more offer you counsel when Mr. Macleod is far more equipped. You've shared more with him than you realize. If you prefer I can give you counsel, and meds, tell you that you have lost it, and send you to the homes like my colleagues, but I firmly believe you would benefit more sharing your experiences with Mr. Macleod." Mr. Schmitz smiled. "Doctor's orders."

Annalise burst out of the office, and stomped to her car, and climbed in. Lachlan climbed into her passenger seat.

"Get out of my car!"

Lachlan buckled his belt and closed his door. "I am not leaving until you talk."

"It's a free world, and I don't have to. Now, get out of my car."

Lachlan crossed his arms. "Free world, I don't have too."

"I will call the cops, Lachlan." Annalise flashed her phone at him, and he took it and threw it into the glove compartment.

"No, you won't. Talk."

Annalise turned to her door and tried to open it, but Lachlan kept locking her in. She turned to him. "Stop it!"

"Free world," he said again, locking the door one last time.

Finally, Annalise got out and walked back to the office. He let her get a few feet away, then went after her, and grabbed her from behind, clamping his hand over her mouth.

"I really didn't want to do this," Lachlan said as he carried her kicking to his car and put her in the back. He'd just installed the cage for Bru, his Irish wolfhound, and locked the door, and climbed into the car, and peeled out of the parking lot.

Annalise screamed and kicked at the window and cage. "Let me out Lachlan, I swear I will press charges for kidnapping!"

"No, you won't," Lachlan said highly confident she wouldn't, and she actually believed she wouldn't, much to her frustration. "Now, talk."

"You first," Annalise told him pouting, and Lachlan growled and turned down a dirt path and stopped the car.

Lachlan turned and looked at her. "Follow me." He

unlocked the back, and climbed out of the car, and down the path. Annalise looked around. She could run, but it would likely take a while to get to her car. Thunder rolled overhead, and Annalise slammed the car door, and ran after Lachlan, not wanting to be left alone.

They walked for an hour when Lachlan finally stopped. Annalise looked around. It was a valley, green and mountainous. She crossed her arms.

"You told me to follow you to the middle of nowhere?"

"This is the Cuillin, the battle of Coire Na Creiche was fought here," Lachlan told her.

"Battle of..Co..coo.." Annalise tried to pronounce

"Coire Na Creiche," Lachlan said, his Scottish accent thick.

"What does that have to do with you... Us?"

"In 1601, below Brauch na Frithe, the clan Macleod, and MacDonald fought their last feud." Lachlan closed his eyes as if he felt the men who died here. "It was bitter, and many a man died."

"What started the war?" Annalise asked.

"Who started the war?" he corrected.

"What is it with you Scotsman, why must someone always start a war?" Annalise scoffed. "You'd think you all would have had enough."

"It was a woman," he growled, and Annalise frowned. "Her name was Margaret, and she was the sister of the Macleod chief. She and the son of the MacDonald chief fell in love with one another." Lachlan looked out over the hills. "They were hand fasted for a year, and a day on condition that she produce a male heir, and then they were to be married."

"Did she have a son?" Annalise asked, not liking where his story was headed.

"No, and to make matters worse, she lost her eyesight in

one eye, and so the chief put her on a one-eyed horse, with a one-eyed servant of his, and a one-eyed dog. The chief loved to stir trouble, and sent her home, and in doing so angered the chief of the Macleod." He looked at her. "The MacDonald slaughtered all the Macleod chieftain's men."

"That's horrible."

"Aye, but if the chieftains had only stopped to listen instead of feud, so many lives would've been spared." Lachlan winced. "I thought the same when I fought alongside the American troops in Iraq."

Annalise looked at him in shock. "You were a soldier?"

"Aye, and I thought peace could fix everything." Lachlan looked back at the Cuillin. "But like the Macleod and MacDonald who hoped Margaret and her man would end their feud, I too made a mistake and cost men their lives." A lone tear slid down his cheek, and he wiped it away. "I deserved no metals after my friends passed. They had died in vain, and since then I am paying for those deaths."

"It wasn't your fault, it was war, death and war work hand in hand. It wasn't Margaret's fault for what happened between the clans either. She'd been infertile, and a sickness likely blinded her. Your experience and hers are not anyone's faults, except maybe those that started the wars."

Lachlan smiled. "That's what I like about you lass, you're smart, and so sure of the world around you. But you, like me, let your past consume you, as Margaret likely let hers consume herself." He looked at her. "You don't realize how much one can hold inside, it's good to talk, and let what's begging to come out, out."

"Even with someone you made a mistake with, and angry at for no reason?"

"Aye, even then."

"Ok, you might want to get comfortable, this wouldn't be talk for a picnic."

"Go ahead, and talk. The Cuillin is beautiful, but hardly a cheery place for a picnic," Lachlan said, and Annalise gave him a grateful smile.

Manna watched the couple below her and smiled. Things were going smoothly now, and she was sure she'd get the full fate spot in no time, as long as Destiny followed through on her end of the bargain. There was only one problem in her human's paths, and that was a witch who called herself Snow. The little fate in training stood and waved a purple hand, instantly transporting herself to Destiny's throne. Her sisters stood on each side, each with their own colors and paths. They bowed low, with smiles on their faces.

"Mother." She bowed, and looked up at the goddess mother of fate, and sometimes the Tuatha dé Danann.

CHAPTER TWELVE

AFTER THEIR LITTLE JAUNT TO THE CUILLIN, AND LEARNING A little about Lachlan's military past, Annalise finally felt her anger toward him dissipate a little, and felt respect for what he had been through, and how he had dealt with it. It was enough for her to finally open up a little about Joseph, and she had to admit, it felt good. Superb, not just to get it out in the open, but to get the anger, and the pent-up emotions out. A weight that was finally lifted from her shoulders, and Lachlan just sat beside her and listened. He didn't show any emotion and didn't interrupt her, just sat there listening and comforting her as she cried.

Dr. Schmitz was correct in assuming that she needed a shoulder to cry on after all those years and thank God she could trust Lachlan. He was different, not in a bad way, no he was a bad boy still, but he was a bad boy with a soft spot, and now she could see that if she allowed it to happen, Lachlan Macleod would be around forever, and likely take very good care of her now, and in the future.

Lachlan tried to keep his eyes on the road as he drove. Beside him in the passenger seat, Annalise was silent.

Mayhap brooding over her past with Joseph, the man was a bastard; she had been through abuse daily and humiliated in the end. It made him wonder if maybe her father, James knew exactly what had gone on and hadn't lifted a finger for his daughter. If he had known her then, he would have beat the shit out of Joseph Declan for even daring to lay his hands on Annalise O'Callaghan. A woman like her should be treated with respect, and given the world, and that was what he hoped he could do. If she would give him a chance, he could show her how she should be treated and give her the future, he knew she craved even though she hadn't told him anything about what she wanted for the future. What could he do to show her he could give her those unspoken things, and what would he need to?

"Is it possible you are mistaken Manna?" Lanna, Manna's next youngest sister, asked as the three sister fates in training walked the halls of Destiny's grand castle.

"I am not. It was the witch Yisarale, and she has called herself Snow," Manna told her.

"Defiling Snow White and the Seven Dwarves, how despicable," Edith, Manna and Lanna's youngest sister said with a sad tone in her voice.

"She is Snow White, just not the way the Grimm brothers made her out to be," Manna said.

Destiny, the mother goddess of fate, and the Tuatha dé Danann, had told the three girls so. The witch had threatened the brothers and made them spin their tales of her under great duress. A child or two had lost their lives, and the brothers were told they wouldn't have a future if they didn't give Yisarale what she wanted. Now they had to deal with her, or rather Destiny did, and since Yisarale was as much alive in the future as she was in the past, Manna would find it hard to keep Lachlan and Annalise on their paths without the witch breaking them apart.

"What do we do Manna?" Edith asked biting her nails

"Trust in the goddess mother, she will lead us and our humans. Yisarale will not get away with her crimes."

"Pfft, she has gotten away with them for centuries. What makes us think she won't this time?" Lanna said, making Edith whine.

Manna looked at them both and shook her head, then walked ahead to get away from them. She snapped her fingers and transported to Skye Ink just as Lachlan and Annalise pulled into the driveway. Manna bit her lower lip, and wondered just how much she as a fate in training could do for them, and concocted a plan that even Yisarale could not even break. It would be risky, but her humans were worth it, and damn it, so was the full-time fates position she so craved.

Lachlan and Annalise began work promptly once they pulled up and climbed out of the car. Lachlan had five clients, each was college kids from St. Andrews looking for some lame tattoo. Annalise felt sorry for Lachlan because each of the kids were young females, barely twenty, and they all wanted him to tattoo Jessica Rabbit onto some part of their bodies. Jessica Rabbit, honestly, the character was hot as hell, but hardly material for the twenty something's that would likely come to regret it later on in their lives.

Annalise watched as one girl rubbed herself "accidentally" against Lachlan's arm with one of her breasts, and she realized with a curse that she was jealous that the young twenty-year-old bitch was messing with him. She even walked over to them and spilt some Dr. Pepper on her just so she could get back at her. Annalise smiled when she got a glare from the twenty-year-old and a bright smile from Lachlan. Great, he now knew she was jealous of the younger meat and actually liked him. No, like was too small a word, she wanted him, yes wanted. Inside her, around her, and forever with her, only her and no one else. They only had sex that one night in his apartment, but he had actually taken a part of her with him, and she was only just beginning to see what that part was.

Lachlan finished up Vickie's tattoo and pawned her off onto Ivy before she could rub him once more. Honestly, if the girl kept doing it, he'd have to kick her out of the shop with her little friends and ban them. They were lucky he was even willing to tattoo some of them without real id's and that he hadn't turned them in for their fake ones. He looked at Annalise, who stood next to Ivy, learning the duties for her new job as Skye Ink's new receptionist. It was good to know that she would work in his shop.

It gave him the opportunity to fix the situation between them and show her how much he had to give to her. He'd seen the jealousy on her face, and how she had spilled just a little of her Dr. Pepper on Vickie earlier. His little vixen was claiming what was hers, and damn it, it felt good to be claimed! Lachlan knew not to get his hopes up, but how could he not, she was his, he knew. Hell, he'd known the first time he had met her on that plane on their way to Scotland. There was nothing anyone or anything that could stop him from making her his, and whether she liked it or not, she had made him hers and that was that. Lachlan smiled at Annalise who smiled back at him, Vickie glowered at them both, and slammed her money down on the glass reception desk and stomped out. He chuckled and walked past her and into the back to look for his next client's folder.

Annalise watched his sexy ass as he walked and felt the burn between her legs when she thought of how that ass looked when he fucked her. She felt a tap on her shoulder, and looked at Ivy who held a bouquet with a card, a strange look on her heavily pierced face. Ivy looked at the guy who had given them to her as he left the shop.

"Lachlan most likely," Ivy answered her unspoken question.

"Why would he send me flowers, he has been with me the whole day?"

Ivy shrugged. "Why do men do anything?" She walked to the back, leaving Annalise alone with the bouquet and card.

Annalise's heart sped up as she opened the card. Lachlan, if it had been Lachlan who sent the flowers, he was a better man than she ever thought he was, a thoughtful one, and he already knew her favorite. Heather and lilies. She froze as she stared down at the card.

Remember Baby,

I will love you forever until death. You're mine, and you will pay for what you have done to me. You will never be happy, as long as I am never happy.

Annalise felt her knees go weak, and she suddenly saw herself falling, but this time Lachlan was there to catch her, and beside him Kieran, Brendon, Aiden, and Ivy all crowded around her.

"What happened?" Lachlan demanded, and she gave him the card.

Lachlan read it, and crumpled it up with a growl, and went to throw it but Aiden tore it from his fist, and he and the others read it.

"That bastard!" Brendon said, punching the floor with his fist. "I will kill him if he ever shows his fucking face."

"Who is this from?" Ivy asked Annalise.

"Joseph Declan," a female voice answered from the doorway to Skye Ink. The group turned and Annalise bolted up from Lachlan's arms and around Brendon, Aiden, and Ivy and froze when she saw a beaten Elspeth leaning on the doorjamb for support.

"Elspeth!" she cried out and ran to the other woman and helped her to a seat.

Aiden watched them both, and his fists clenched when she passed. The bruises and bloody nose were enough to enrage a man, but her entire body from her head to her neck and arms were covered in bruises, and cigarette burns. He growled, and beside him Kieran, and Brendon did too. What kind of man did this to her, and if he was around, was he ready to be castrated?

Annalise sat her in one of the tattoo chairs, and grabbed a paper towel, wetted it and dabbed at Elspeth's cuts.

"What happened?"

"He beat me, burned me." Elspeth showed her arms where the fresh cigarette burns lingered. "You were right all along. He was no good, and I don't understand why I ever left with him. He's angry that you left Seattle, that you dropped off the face of the world. I didn't even know where you were, until I saw your dad, and he helped me get away from Joseph."

"Did James get you to a hospital for those?"

"Yes, but I left. I can't stay there, Annalise, not when I know Joseph is looking for me. I am sorry. I am afraid I may have led him to you. I am such an idiot," Elspeth cried. Aiden walked into the room and knelt down in front of her and handed her his handkerchief.

"You are not an idiot, he is a bastard that has no balls. You can stay with me until we get this cleared up." He looked at Annalise, who gave him a shocked look. "What?"

Annalise shook her head. "I just never heard you speak this much and didn't expect for you to take her in."

"He usually doesn't," Ivy said. "You should see him when we are at home, drives me nuts. But what are brothers for?"

"Your brother and sister?"

"Aye, been that way since I first met him. Different moms though," Ivy said with a small smile. "Dad got around really well." She giggled perversely and looked at Elspeth. "We will take care of you, don't you worry about a thing. Joseph will not get near you, and if he does, I own various swords and guns. Any one of them will suffice."

Elspeth gave a small smile, not knowing exactly how to take the pierced woman, and then looked at Aiden. He seemed to genuinely care, and for the first time in months she felt safe, and knew he and his sister would keep her that way until she could find another way.

"I will stay with you," she told him, and Aiden grunted. Elspeth looked at Ivy. "Do you have a license to teach me how to shoot one of those guns?"

"I can teach you," Aiden said surprising, everyone in the room. "A woman has a right to defend herself." He stood and pulled her out of the seat and into his arms, making her squeal and shrink when his tattooed arms bulged with muscle. Aiden looked at them all. "I am taking her to my house, my shift tonight is over Lachlan, tell my clients to reschedule or go to Brendon if they want their tattoos."

"I will call James okay, Elspeth?" Annalise asked the woman who was once her friend as Aiden carried her out.

"Okay," Elspeth said, not sure what to say or do as Aiden carried her out of the parlor and to his car.

Annalise watched the couple leave and felt fear for herself and Elspeth. More for Elspeth because Joseph could have killed her. She turned to go back to reception and bumped into Lachlan.

"He won't get near you, if he does, I have no problems with killing him," Lachlan said, his voice deep and threatening. It actually gave her chills.

Annalise lifted onto her tiptoes and pressed her lips to his. "I know you would, but I am not afraid of Joseph." She lied, and Lachlan's forest green eyes flashed. "Alright, I am afraid of him, but I know I will be safe. Besides, I have you, Brendon, Aiden, and Kieran as my Avengers. All I have to say is assembled and there you all will be."

"Assemble? Avengers?" Lachlan asked moving his head side to side in confusion.

"You know, Nick Fury, Captain America, Thor?" Annalise asked. When he said nothing, she gasped. "Oh, we are so going to rectify this situation quickly." Annalise turned and went to walk back to the desk to finish her tasks for the day.

Annalise called her father on her next break and set Elspeth up with him. He was not happy, but Elspeth would leave early in the morning to her new home in Scotland, complete with an investigation team to monitor her. No blame there. He wanted to make sure Elspeth wasn't conning anyone and working with Joseph to get back at his daughter.

She looked around the corner from her desk and to the back where Lachlan sat in the manager's office, his door wide open and welcoming. She could hear him talking to someone over the phone, most likely a former client asking questions about future tattoos, or Aiden talking to him about Elspeth's current situation and Joseph's involvement in it. He was determined to keep her safe, and although she was pleased he was being protective, she also felt like he was being way too protective. She hadn't seen Joseph in a while, and she wasn't worried about him coming after her, she was worried more about Elspeth. Joseph had beaten her, and she hoped that was all he had done to her old best friend.

Annalise heard Lachlan say goodbye to whoever he had

been talking too and watched as he walked into his artist room. She looked out the front door to make sure no one pulled up, stood, and walked back to his room. She froze just before she got to his door, and inhaled. Tonight would be the night. She was going to get her tattoo, last time she was afraid, but tonight after finding Elspeth, and hearing of Joseph's coming to Scotland, she owed herself something to show her courage, and Lachlan was the man to tattoo her. Annalise entered the room, Lachlan's back was facing her.

"Lachlan?"

Lachlan turned and looked at her. "Aye?" He looked worried. "Are you okay?"

Annalise nodded and that worry melted away. He was on edge as much as she was about Joseph. Maybe asking him for the tattoo would help the both of them.

"What is it lass, is there a client?"

"No," Annalise said, putting her arms behind her back, and walked toward the seat, and eyed it before looking at him. "I am ready now."

Lachlan stared at her, muttering what she had just said, and then realization dawned on him.

"Sit down, Annalise." She sat down in the oversized chair, and he rolled his chair to her, and sat. "Are you certain you want the tattoo now?" Annalise nodded, and Lachlan stood. "It's forever, you can back out right now, and no one will fault you, not even Ivy."

"I understand Lachlan," Annalise said, raising her chin defiantly. "I will not back out, forever is what I want."

Lachlan felt his heart race at those last words 'Forever is what I want'.

"I will get the design you wanted the first time."

"No." Annalise said, and Lachlan looked at her. confused once more.

"No?"

"I don't want that anymore, I want you to design whatever you want for me. I want only your work on my body, not something I came up with."

Lachlan smiled and gave her a nod. "I have the perfect tattoo." He walked back to his cabinet, and got out a couple of ink bottles, needles, his tattoo machines, and a large paper towel, and set up the table next to her. He opened a drawer beneath it, and pulled out a tube of ointment, and three small cups, and opened the bottles of ink after giving them a good shake. Lachlan filled one with black, another with red, and one more with blue, and then put the ink back where they belonged.

He sat back down on the chair, and set up his machine, inserting the needles, and wrapping it in plastic before hooking it up with two prongs that almost looked like they could power a small battery. Lachlan moved his foot to a small peddle by his chair in the shape of a small dragon and tested the machine. It buzzed, and he nodded, sat it down, and took out a razor from the drawer.

"Which arm do you want the tattoo on?" He asked her.

"Um..." Annalise looked at the mirror to her right, behind him. "Right arm please, I want to watch."

"Right it is." He shaved her arm with the razor, then pulled gloves from a box, and put them on, and dipped his fingers in some ointment. He rubbed it on her arm, picked up his machine, and scooted in close to her.

"What about the stencil?" she asked.

"Don't need one for this, my imagination is all I need, lass," Lachlan told her as pressed on his peddle and barely touched her before asking. "How is that?"

"It doesn't hurt, just feels uncomfortable," Annalise said.

"Tell me if it does, and we will take a brief break."

Annalise nodded, and he dipped his machine in the black ink, and outlined a small heart. Annalise watched as the heart took shape and realized that the pain was nothing compared to what she had thought it would feel like. An hour passed, and Lachlan connected the heart to a Celtic knot on both sides, and spread it out around her arm on one side, he had her lay on her back and lift her arm so he could wrap the band under her arm, and to the other side to complete the knot. She winced a little as the needle met with her sensitive flesh and turned her eyes from the mirror to Lachlan's face.

Annalise felt the heat building between her thighs as she stared at Lachlan, remembering that handsome face as he had loomed over her when they had sex the night of their first date. She suddenly knew then as she watched him complete the knot under her arm, and helped her sit up to complete it, that she loved him, and that the night of their first encounter hadn't been a mistake as she had once thought, but something she knew was a long time coming. She smiled at him, and when he finished the outline, and straightened his back, and washed out his machine, Annalise reached out and ran her fingers through his ponytail. Lachlan froze, and stared at her. He saw then the look of love she was showing him and suddenly felt hot and hard all over. His stomach felt like it was doing flip-flops. He grabbed her hand, and squeezed it, before dipping his machine in the red ink, and filled in the heart. Lachlan immediately knew his decision to tattoo his own Celtic love knot on her arm was a good one. She cared for him, and possibly loved him now, and there was no other explanation. It was what he had wanted since the first time he had met her, and he knew then, just as he knew at that moment that she was his, and now she knew it.

It was midnight when he finally finished, and Lachlan proud of his work sat back as Annalise looked it over, smiling brightly as she exclaimed her love for the Celtic band and its heart. Annalise felt like her heart was going to explode. The tattoo was beautiful and fit her so well with its black and blue outlined Celtic knot, and red heart. It was the ultimate feminine tattoo, and Lachlan had executed it so well to fit around her small arm. And all without a stencil!

She turned to look at him, her eyes filled to the brim with unshed tears. She walked over to him and pressed his lips to hers in a passionate kiss. Lachlan pulled her down into his lap, and grabbed her ass as Annalise spread her legs, and pressed herself against him where his penis lay pressing up against his jeans. Annalise moaned and broke the kiss to stare down at him, and Lachlan laughed.

"I take it you love the tattoo a lot?" Lachlan said huskily as he rubbed his hands up and down her back.

"I love it." Annalise said kissing him again. "I love you," she whispered, and Lachlan's entire world slowed, and he looked up at her.

"Say that again?"

"I love you," Annalise told him once more, and Lachlan laughed, and picked her and spun her around the room and Annalise squealed. "I take it that's a good thing?" she asked him when he finally stopped spinning.

"It's the best!" he said to her pulling her into another kiss. "I love you too." He kissed her again. "Say it again." He kissed her. "Say it to me."

"I love you Lachlan Macleod," Annalise panted in between kisses, and Lachlan pushed her up against the wall of his workroom, and kissed her deeply, unclasping her bra, and finding her breasts with his hands. "I love you." She moaned, and Lachlan ground himself against her heat, and Annalise threw her head back in a soft moan. "I want you," she panted, and Lachlan pulled her panties down her legs and unzipped his jeans.

"Say it again," he told her huskily, rubbing himself against her opening with the tip of his penis.

"I love you," she panted, and Lachlan thrust himself inside of her hard and fast. Annalise screamed out. "I Love You!!!"

"Stupid bitch," he muttered as he toppled over the couch. "Teach her to ruin my life."

Joseph Declan looked around at his handy work and smiled. Annalise O'Callaghan's life was going to go downhill quickly, he'd make sure she didn't have a friend or family member to help her ever again. As for Elspeth, well, that bitch could rot for all he cared, he'd used her to hurt Annalise, to control her, he'd failed at that, but he wouldn't fail at this. Not this time. She was going to pay. Joseph emptied the last bit of gas from his gas can and walked to the door. He struck a match and threw it onto the floor. He laughed as he watched pictures, and papers, and soon furniture caught fire. He turned, and walked to her mailbox, took out a small picture he had taken of her, and wrote on it in red marker, kissed it, and put it into the mailbox before he climbed into his vehicle, and watched the house now ablaze disappear in his rearview mirror. He laughed once more when a fire truck and police cars sped passed him. The bitch would come home to find nothing to her name, nothing as he'd had nothing.

Lachlan rubbed Annalise's back as they lay on his bed in his apartment, they had closed Skye Ink at around midnight, and had taken their lovemaking to the apartment, and did it in the kitchen, bathrooms, extra bedrooms, living room where they'd had their first date, and finally bed room. It was three in the morning by the time they had finished. Lachlan kissed

Annalise on her forehead, and she snuggled in close to him, and smiled in sexual satisfaction. Her phone rang, and she sighed, and reached over to the nightstand to pick it up. Annalise frowned at the caller id. It was not a number she recognized at all. She showed it to Lachlan, who frowned as well, and she answered it.

"Hello?"

"Annalise O'Callaghan?" a male voice asked.

"Yes, this is she."

"This is Chief McRae, come meet me at your house. There has been an incident."

Annalise bolted up out of bed, and Lachlan watched from his position on the bed.

"What kind of incident?"

"A fire was started in your home, ma'am." Annalise felt a cold dread course through her to settle in her stomach. "We believe it was arson."

Lachlan stood and walked over to her just as Annalise covered her mouth with her hand. He caught her as her knees buckled.

"I will be over soon, just give me a minute."

"Very well ma'am, I will be waiting."

Annalise hung up the phone and turned to Lachlan. "That was the chief of police. My house caught fire."

Pilanin growled as he looked at what was left of Annalise's home. It was all gone. He kicked a piece of rubble and looked at the chief of police standing next to Annalise, and a man he'd never seen before. He'd felt a strong power coming off the man beside her, and he'd run up to investigate it, and was almost overpowered by what he felt from the man Annalise called Lachlan. They couldn't't see him in this guise, but he could have sworn that Lachlan saw him. It was fleeting and lasted only for a second before he went back to talking to the chief of police. Pilanin learned that a man named Joseph Declan could have started the fire, and he knew from his best friend, James O'Callaghan, that this man was an ex of Annalise's and was significant enough to be labeled as a suspect. Pilanin ran from the scene towards his car parked the next street over and whispered the counter spell that would allow him to become visible again.

He pulled out his keys, but before he could unlock his car, and climb into it he was shocked to find a little girl standing beside his car. Her hair was long and purple, her hands and body, even the clothes she wore were as well, or at least they seemed to be outlined in purple.

"Can I help you?" he asked her.

"Yes, I believe you can, Pilanin of Otherworld."

CHAPTER THIRTEEN

Pilanin stared at the woman, unsure what he was to think of her. She was exquisite and seemed not of this world.

"Who are you?" he asked her.

The woman smiled. "My name is old, and you might not know of me. I am a goddess, come to tell you that Annalise is not in any danger and that she is being watched."

"So says a goddess who won't share her name!" Pilanin snorted. "How do I know you aren't the person who burnt down Annalise O'Callaghan's home?"

"You must trust me," the goddess said.

Pilanin crossed his arms. "Fine, maybe you have some insight, being a so-called goddess, which I still don't believe."

The goddess smirked. "Very well, I shall exhibit my power."

She threw out a hand and concentrated on the ground and dirt. She imagined her fingers were roots, and that they were growing out of the ground. Before long, a tiny plant grew, and before Pilanin could speak it burst forth and bloomed into a rosebush. The scent strong and the roses red as lipstick.

The raw power coming from that bush nearly knocked Pilanin on his ass.

"Now do you believe me?"

Pilanin nodded and said nothing as the goddess continued to tell him about the fire and the man behind it.

Annalise could still hardly believe that her home was now gone. She picked at her chow mien and tried not to think about the things she'd lost. She'd just be grateful for the things she had, like her digital files for her book, and her purse and some clothing and laptop. Truly, this was all she needed, and that was the beauty of it, she could work anywhere. She had a funny feeling who had possibly burned down her new home, and frankly that scared her. Annalise had thought she had finally escaped from Joseph Declan's reach, and that she could move on now. Why couldn't he just leave her alone?

Lachlan walked back into the dining room carrying a bag from Apple. He handed it to her.

"I meant to give this to you last night, but we had to deal with the house and talking to the police. I thought maybe you could use a pick me up," Lachlan explained.

Annalise took the bag and pulled out a tablet, pencil, and case.

"Lachlan, this is too much!" Annalise told him.

"Just accept it Annalise. It's a gift, nothing more."

Annalise nodded and stood. She pulled Lachlan into a hug and gave him a peck on the lips. "This will definitely help me. Thank you."

Lachlan smiled at her and then turned his attention to her food. "You've barely eaten a thing lass."

" I haven't felt like eating since what happened to my

house Lachlan. You'd feel the same if it were your home that burned down," Annalise explained.

"Do you have any idea who could have done it?"

"Oh. Several, and all they trace back to my ex-fiancé. I just don't understand why he'd burn down my house and not just came after me," Annalise explained.

Lachlan frowned. "Perhaps he didn't want to confront you because you are around me?"

Annalise pursed her lips. He had a point. Joseph was always one to be jealous, but that didn't explain why he would likely burn down her house. Joseph was rich, and very classy. It seemed pretty dumb that he'd sacrifice his dignity and reputation just to burn down a home. Something more seemed to be going on and, Annalise didn't know what that could be. She knew that her new home was now gone, and that her father, James, was likely hot on Joseph's trail. The man would be blindsided by the wrath that was James O'Callaghan.

"If that is the case, Annalise, I think you should stay with me. At least until you get back on your feet," Lachlan explained.

Annalise nodded, at least until she got a new home. She didn't like the idea of having to move back in with her father. It would be detailed, and she could not go anywhere without a guard. Maybe with Lachlan, her father wouldn't be so obsessed with her protection.

"Thank you, Lachlan. I think I am going to bed now." With that said, Annalise stood on her tiptoes and gave Lachlan a kiss and retired to his bedroom.

Lachlan cleaned up and thought about what he could do for Annalise. Usually he wouldn't have the woman he was dating or having sex with move in with him, but Annalise was different. He felt complete, and whole when he was with her. So, it didn't matter that she moved in with him, he wanted her here. Hell, he wanted her here forever! But that was too soon, even for him. Not to mention Annalise would likely panic. For now, it was better to just live in the moment, and take it slow. Lachlan retired as well an hour later, pulling Annalise close as he spooned her. He just realized that he could have lost her tonight.

Lachlan smoothed back Annalise's hair and breathed in her scent. She smelled of Vanilla and spice. It soothed him to know that she was there, safe in his arms. Annalise whimpered in her sleep, and Lachlan rubbed her back to comfort her until she calmed down, peaceful again. Lachlan then closed his eyes and fell asleep.

That morning, Annalise and Lachlan sat in the police station waiting to be seen by the detectives. James O'Callaghan sat in a chair in front of them and stared at Lachlan as if he were trying to drill holes into the younger man. Truth was, Janes had become suspicious of Lachlan since all the bad seemed to happen when he was around, and it certainly felt like that. Even Lachlan had to admit it.

James then turned his attention back to the officers, and Lachlan sighed in relief. The officers spoke about the possibility of Joseph Declan having committed arson, but that they had very little evidence to suggest that Annalise's ex-fiancé was even in Scotland. It was all certainly maddening.

"Do you have a place to stay Miss O'Callaghan?" asked one detective.

"She can stay with me," Lachlan blurted out, and that got him a suspicious look from James. "That is, if Annalise wants too."

"I would love to," Annalise answered. She did not want to go back to the mansion and stay cooped up with bodyguards on duty night and day. Knowing her father well, Annalise knew that's exactly what would happen.

Lachlan felt his heart swell and his chest puffed out in

pride. Annalise had chosen him over going to her father's home where he'd likely not be able to visit or hold her in his arms. Because James O'Callaghan was suspicious, Lachlan believed he could very well be the type to protect his daughter and interrogate him.

"Well, you have some clothing at the mansion, so if you need I can have Jasper bring them to you," James told them, surprising them as well.

It was strange that her father would readily accept her decision. After what happened between her and Joseph, her father had become very protective. She wondered what could have changed because James O'Callaghan never shied away from protecting his own.

Lachlan helped Annalise pack what she could find at the mansion, and then they moved her into his home. It was the first time Lachlan had ever moved in with a girl, and he was determined not to screw it up. Annalise set up her clothing in the space in the closet and drawers Lachlan had cleared out for her in his dresser.

"I guess this just got official," Annalise said after she put the last of her clothing away.

"Babe, it has always been official since the first day I saw you on the plane," Lachlan said pulling Annalise into his arms and bringing his lips down onto hers in a long kiss.

Lachlan broke the kiss and rubbed her arms. "What's wrong, lass?"

Annalise shook her head. "Nothing, just thinking about the fire and all of my things, I don't understand why he had to come after me. I left him, and he was perfectly okay with that."

"Sometimes a person's personality doesn't come out until much later. It is important to understand that you are here and safe."

Annalise nodded. "Thank you Lachlan, for everything. I think I am going to go take a nap, it's been a long day."

Lachlan nodded and watched as Annalise walked into his room and closed the door behind her. He worried that Joseph, her ex, was going to find her while he was at work. He didn't feel comfortable leaving her alone, even for a minute. He took out his phone and texted Kieran, asking him if he could come over and stay with Annalise while she slept. His brother seemed annoyed but agreed to come over and stay for the remainder of his shift at Skye Ink. A moment later, Kieran walked into the apartment.

"I wish I could stay, I really thank you for this," Lachlan told Kieran.

"Anything, do you have any news on the person who burned down Annalise's home?"

"They believe it was a man named Joseph Declan. He was her ex-fiancé," Lachlan explained to his younger brother.

Kieran frowned. "Why would he care enough to burn down her house?"

Lachlan shrugged, to be honest he wasn't sure why Joseph would go after Annalise now rather than when they'd been together. All Lachlan knew was Annalise was not well emotionally, and this news had messed with her emotionally, and scared her. What was in it for Joseph Declan?

CHAPTER FOURTEEN

Joseph Declan sat at the bar, a drink in hand. He'd wanted to get even with Annalise and show her that no matter how far she went, she'd never escape him. She was his, and the man she was with was of no consequence to Joseph. He'd just use Elspeth, a friend of Annalise's and his current lover to get to her. Elspeth would do anything for him. If she didn't, he would reveal her cheating ways, and that she had slept with him for money for her kid. He hoped burning down the home was enough to scare Annalise and show her he would do anything to get her back. She would be his no matter what.

Joseph took a drink of his brandy and smoked some of his cigar. He turned his attention to the crowd in the bar and watched as a younger woman, beautiful beyond imagination, walked over to him. Her hair was long and dark, her skin like cream, and her lips a dark red. She smiled at him as she came to sit next to him. Joseph gave her a smile and waived down the bartender.

"What are you having?" he asked the woman.

"If I am lucky, you but I will settle for a rum and coke,"

the woman said.

Joseph could feel her, and his excitement built up at the thought of sharing a bed with this woman. Something about her seemed right, and he was very interested in her.

"I am Joseph, Joseph Declan," he introduced himself.

"Snow." She grabbed his hand and placed it upon her pale cheek. "I am wondering if you could do something for me."

Joseph felt himself being drawn into her. "What would you want done?"

Snow smiled. "A small thing really, but I have a friend who needs to be knocked down a notch, and I thought maybe you could do that for me."

Joseph stared at Snow and looked into her eyes. He was hooked, line and sinker! He was hers now.

"Anything you wish, my queen," Joseph said to her, kissing the back of the hand.

Snow smiled and motioned for Joseph to follow her as she stood and led him out of the bar.

Annalise went through her files and found that she had saved her work to great relief. She hadn't lost everything in the fire and work could continue on the book. She booted up her tablet and turned on the keyboard she'd found at the end of the bed from Lachlan and opened her book and typed.

An hour later, Annalise had finished two chapters, and poured out all the frustration and grief that she had felt onto the page. Annalise took a break for lunch and walked through the living room to go to the kitchen and froze when she saw Kieran asleep on the couch. Annalise tried to sneak past, but Kieran burst out laughing.

"You're a poor excuse for a quiet person," Kieran told her.

Annalise shook her head. "Why are you here?"

"Waiting on Lachlan. He went into work and has yet to come home," Kieran said.

"Have you really been here all day?" Annalise asked in shock.

"Lachlan was worried about you, and so I came over to put his worries to ease."

Annalise frowned and clenched her fists. "He sent you as my babysitter!?"

Kieran's eyes widened when he realized what he'd just started. He jumped up from the couch and ran after Annalise when she spun on her heel and walked outside as Lachlan was pulling up.

"You asshole!" Annalise told Lachlan as he exited the vehicle. "Can't trust me enough to take care of myself? First the tablet, and now a babysitter?"

Lachlan raised his hands in the air in surrender. "I am sorry lass, I was just trying to take care of you, and Kieran would be the best sacrifice for your devilish ex. I mean come on look at him no man could resist that fist!"

"That's not funny Lachlan. I need you to trust me and know that I will be fine by myself. That's why I left my father's home. You can't imagine what it's like to have an entourage of babysitters on retainer."

Lachlan hadn't taken that into consideration and hadn't realized that James O'Callaghan would employ people to watch his daughter when he couldn't. He also couldn't imagine how she must have felt every time she found a hired man following her.

"Ah lass, I am so sorry," Lachlan said, and he pulled her into his arms.

"I'll be leaving now," Kieran told the couple, feigning like he was about to get sick.

Lachlan pulled Annalise into the house as Kieran left them. He kissed her deeply as he pushed her up against the door. Annalise broke the kiss panting. Lachlan looked at her as he picked her up and wrapped her legs around his waist, kissing her passionately and deeply. He ground his hips between her thighs and let her feel how much she affected him. Annalise moaned into Lachlan's mouth and slid her hands into his shirt to trace his muscled chest, abs, and then around and into his pants to grab onto his ass as he ground against her. She needed to feel his skin on hers, and she wanted to feel him inside of her.

Lachlan let Annalise come up for air and threw her onto her belly on the arm of the couch. He yanked her jeans and panties down in quick succession and his own just as fast. He entered her fast, and Annalise let out a scream of pleasure as Lachlan increased the speed and kept thrusting hard and deep within her. He exploded just as she came, and they both collapsed over the couch to catch their breath.

It felt like a betrayal, Lachlan had gone against her, and taken Annalise into his arms and bed again. Why did she have to be the one cast out? She was more beautiful and far sexier than that woman. Snow pouted as she waited for Joseph to finish up with his shower. Lachlan would be hers. The mirror had showed her, and the mirror was never wrong. It predicted that she was beautiful and had told her that her stepmother was going to kill her.

Snow watched as Joseph Declan came out of the bathroom naked and felt the arousal build between her legs. She motioned for him to come to her with her finger, and he climbed on top of her, and slipped into her wet canal. Snow moaned and raked her nails down his back as he thrust deep inside her. After their intense love making, she sent Joseph out in pursuit of Annalise. She needed to know more about her and wanted to torment her before she attacked. Playing with the prey, she called it. Soon Lachlan would be hers, just as the mirror said, and she would have her happily ever after.

Joseph watched as Annalise and Lachlan left the house and followed them to the store. He followed close behind as they shopped for clothing for her. Joseph felt such an overwhelming anger that she was with Lachlan rather than with him. It didn't matter that he had his Queen Snow. Annalise was his and had always been since he first met her, and now he must break up the relationship with the Scotsman. Stupid man. What did he have that Joseph didn't have?

Two dresses, five blouses and three trousers later, Annalise walked out of the dressing room and putting her new clothing picks back into the cart.

"Hello Annalise." The voice had Annalise freezing and turning on her heel, her heart going up into her throat.

"Joseph, what are you doing here?"

Joseph scoffed. "See you upgraded fast. Wasn't I enough for you?"

Annalise turned on her heel to run, but Joseph grabbed her arm and slammed her against the clothing racks to crash through. Annalise screamed, and that alerted the staff of the store, and Lachlan who came running, tackling Joseph to the ground before he could drag Annalise by her hair. Lachlan punched Joseph and knocked him out as the police pulled him off the man. They handcuffed Lachlan and called for an ambulance for Joseph. When they came, he was handcuffed to the bed and wheeled away.

"Take the car home lass, I'll be out soon," Lachlan told Annalise as they looked her over.

"I'll call my father, I promise."

Lachlan smiled and went willingly with the officers. They questioned Annalise as their fellow officers took Lachlan from the scene. After she'd answered all their questions, Annalise called her father. Lachlan would be out quickly. They won't be able to keep him overnight, and the worst he would get was a ticket and a slap on the wrist. Joseph had a far unique experience to be had.

Lachlan walked out of the back room of the station and found James O' Callaghan waiting for him.

"Sorry to be havin' this happen when it should be for meet the parents' night," Lachlan told him.

James smirked and shook his head. "Can't rightly be angry with you with that ignorant excuse of an apology." He nodded towards the room they held Joseph. "Anything said about why he attacked my daughter?"

"No, but seemed to me he was in a stupor when he attacked her. He seems really confused as well, and I am not sure that he isn't confused right now. He doesn't act like he knows what's going on and that's information that I have overheard from the officers when they passed my room," Lachlan explained.

James nodded. "You should leave and go to Annalise, she is not doing so well with you getting arrested. There is something you should know about my daughter Lachlan and that is my daughter can, and will blame herself for all of this. She used to be very strong, but he broke her down and she became the victim." James brought out a cigar and lit it, a show to all the officers that passed that rules were made for him to break them. No one said a thing, they all knew James O'Callahan. "Keep your eye on her and don't let her go."

" I don't plan too. In fact, wanted to speak to you about that."

Lachlan returned to Annalise later that night and made love to her and made the most difficult decision of his life, all in one night.

An hour later, Lachlan awoke to pain from his back. He climbed out of bed and walked to his bathroom where a sheet mirror hung. He turned the lights on and found his back and legs covered in blood. Lachlan turned and got a glimpse at his back and got concerned and then went into shock as he watched a tattoo being carved into his back.

The pain, Lachlan grimaced as he felt the burning intensity on his back as he hobbled towards the fairy pools. Not sure why he'd drive himself here, of all places. This was a place he wanted to propose to Annalise at. But damn, he'd had many tattoos during his life, but this felt like he was being burned alive. Dots swam before his eyes as a thousand needles slid in and out of his back. Lachlan fell onto his knees as the pain got intense. He heaved and lost whatever food he'd eaten that night.

The fairy pool loomed before him, a large pool with an underwater bridge. The same pool that he and Annalise shared a night of lovemaking. The happiest place and time of his life, a woman who loved him truly and completely. He remembered it had a waterfall in the background, and the water before him seemed to glow in the moonlight, clear and with a bit of a pale blue hue to it.

He would definitely propose to her here. His pain intensified and Lachlan screamed.

He felt the urge to walk into the cool waters of the fairy pools. Lachlan felt the cool water as it soothed the burning, but not before he felt the hand grab his ankle and pulled him under.

CHAPTER FIFTEEN

Lachlan tried to kick his legs to find whatever was holding him and connected with nothing but water. He could feel his lungs burning as he was drug further under the water. Lachlan screamed, and water rushed into his mouth and into his lungs. He passed out just as the water spit him out into a cavern with many carved Celtic knot work all over the walls. A young man, about Lachlan's age came forward and knelt down beside the unconscious Lachlan.

He placed his hands over Lachlan, and sent healing energy within him, and Lachlan coughed up water and took a gulp of air. He tried to get his bearings and stared at the man sitting beside him. The pain in his back struck higher again, and Lachlan screamed as a pair of black and white wings bust forth from his back.

"Welcome, brother," the man said to him finally.

Lachlan collapsed onto his belly, his wings twitching with the remnants of the pain. What the hell had just happened! Why had he suddenly sprouted wings! Fucking wings!?

"You're probably wondering what has just happened," the man said as if reading his mind. "You're a late bloomer Lachlan, and you have just come into your Tuatha dé Danann blood."

Lachlan felt the bile rise into his throat, and silently cursed his family. Had they angered the fae or had a child with one? What the fuck?

"We haven't had a late bloomer in a long time. Come to think of it, we haven't had one of our own be shrouded in such secrecy. The Seelie court will not like this, but I suppose Father will be happy to know that I have finally found you after all these centuries," the man continued to say.

"Father?" Lachlan croaked. "My father is human"

"Your adopted mother and father are human. Your real mother is indeed human, but your real father is a proud Tuatha dé Danann," the man corrected.

Lachlan cursed again and tried to push down the anger and panic that reared its ugly head. Just how much did his mom and dad keep from him?

"My name is Ashlar, and I am the son of Llyr and prince of the Unseelie court. For the human part of my name you may call me Ethan, I think it's fair I give you my fae name as a gesture of goodwill and trust," Ethan told him. "From now on you will call me Ethan."

"You called me brother," Lachlan said. "You are not my brother."

"I am unfortunately, and if you are to survive, you would do well to remember that. Unless you'd like to keep to yourself and risk being caught."

Lachlan grimaced and flexed a wing and found that the pain had eased somewhat.

"Do I really have a choice?" Lachlan asked. "You are fae, and I know nothing about your laws."

Ethan nodded. "Yes, but you are brethren I can let you slide to navigate the human world and ours. You've been gone for so long and you'll need to come home to us, eventually. "

Lachlan frowned at him. "I am not going anywhere. Not with you, fae."

Ethan sighed. "Very well, but when Father comes for you, do not blame me for your actions." He helped Lachlan to his feet and helped keep him steady. "And please remember that you are fae as well. If you use that word, then you talk of yourself with that disdain and that is unbecoming of a fae prince."

"I really don't care, and what in the hell do I do with these damn wings?" Lachlan asked.

Ethan laughed. "I knew you'd say that, and the wings will disappear into the tattoo on your back and don't worry, it will no longer hurt, and you can call upon them when you need them. "

"That's good to know," Lachlan said and watched in amazement as they seemed to shift from the cavern to find themselves outside by the fairy pool. "What the hell?"

Ethan laughed again. "We don't always use our wings. We can transport ourselves to other places as long as we are close by them. An adaptation we have to keep from being found."

No wonder they were fae and not very trustworthy, and most of the Celtic countries feared and respected them. Hell, a whole highway had was rerouted because there was a hawthorn tree there.

"Why me?" Lachlan asked Ethan, and the man shrugged.

"You were born fae but kept from us, and I have no answers for you on that," Ethan explained. "The only one who knows those answers is Llyr the Unseelie King."

Lachlan groaned. Fae blood and the Unseelie King was his father! This had to be a very bizarre dream, and soon Annalise will wake him up from it. Anytime now but no.

Instead, Ethan was helping him lay on his couch and covering him up. His wings had long disappeared and the pain in his back had gone away.

"You'll likely wake up with a fuzzy memory. Don't worry, this is normal and it will all come back little by little," Ethan told him.

Lachlan shook his head and closed his eyes. "When I wake up, this will be a dream and you'll be in my imagination fae."

Ethan laughed. "You hope."

Annalise woke up that morning to find Lachlan staring at himself in the mirror, a set of giant Celtic wings tattooed on his back.

"When did you get that?" Annalise asked

"Last night apparently." He couldn't possibly tell her what happened last night as she wouldn't likely believe him. He'd have to figure out a way to tell her, but it would likely wait until after he'd proposed to her. If he was fae, he wanted to make sure she was his before he told her anything. She was American however and didn't have the same beliefs as the Celts did. Maybe telling her would be the best thing to do. She was an author as well, so her imagination was strong and healthy.

"Can I talk to you but not here?" Lachlan asked Annalise.

Annalise nodded, concerned about what it could be and worried that Lachlan was breaking up with her. An hour later, after getting dressed, Lachlan and Annalise took a drive back to the fairy pools.

Lachlan looked around the pool and pointed to the Celtic knot on the side of the manmade bridge.

"That wasn't here before Annalise, and there is a reason."

"Alright." Annalise said. "Lachlan, just tell me you are breaking up with me."

Lachlan sighed and knelt down onto one knee and

brought out the ring box and ring. Annalise covered her mouth and tried not to cry.

"Will you do me the honor of being my wife?"

Annalise nodded and let him put the ring on her finger. "We haven't been together that long Lachlan, are you sure?"

"As sure as the stars that shine in your eyes, my love." Lachlan pulled her to him and pressed his lips to hers in a kiss.

"As sure as the stars...Oh how lovely," a female voice said behind the couple. They both turned to find the woman from Eilean Donan Castle standing there. Her skin was pale, her hair long and black, contrasting with her red lips. "Too bad you won't be having a wedding."

Lachlan felt an anger build, and his tattoo burned as his wings appeared. He wasn't in any pain, this time it felt like a small sunburn. His wings burst forth, ripping his shirt. He heard Annalise's scream and looked at her just in time to find Joseph Declan walk out of the trees with a gun pointed at her. Lachlan growled and flapped his wings, which stopped the man in his tracks. Joseph just stared at Lachlan as he tried to process that the man had wings. This gave Lachlan an opening to take flight, grab Declan and throw him and his gun into the fairy pool.

"Oh, bravo, my dearest," said the woman

Lachlan flew back to Annalise and stepped in front of her.

"I am not your dearest. What do you want?" Lachlan asked her.

The woman pouted. "The stars, give me the stars, Lachlan son of Llyr and claim your rightful place as my King!

Lachlan shook his head. "Sorry, you're not my type."

The woman's pout went from serene to anger and rage the next, and she shouted. "No one rejects Snow of the White Hills!"

Snow lept into action, and Lachlan braced himself as she

collided with him, all claws and fury. Lachlan threw Snow off and into a tree, not realizing his newfound strength. He turned to Annalise and scooped her into her arms and flew her to the safety of his car.

"Go home, I'll handle things here," Lachlan told her, giving her a kiss.

"What the hell is going on? Why the hell do you have wings?" Annalise asked, panic in her voice.

" I'll explain later. Keep this safe for us," Lachlan told her and handed her his ring box.

Annalise nodded and gasped, and Lachlan realized that Snow had found them. He pushed Annalise into the car. "Drive away as fast as you can."

Annalise shook her head. "Go with me, Lachlan. We can go to the police."

Lachlan laughed sadly. "I don't think the police will help with this one, my love."

Snow howled, and Lachlan turned as she came for him. Lachlan threw Snow to the ground and turned to Annalise. "Go now!" He slammed the car door and Annalise started it and sped off. When she was a few yards away she parked it and ran back to Lachlan and the scene unfolding before the world.

Lachlan circled around now as she circled him.

"You're mine Lachlan, can't you see we belong together?"

"I don't even know you, but what I know is that you send every hair on my body up straight. I can sense that you are unnatural, just as I am," Lachlan explained.

Snow lunged at him and grabbed onto him. "You will be mine Lachlan, son of Llyr. I will make sure of that."

Lachlan tried to fight the woman off, but she was unnaturally strong, and he knew he didn't stand a chance since he knew nothing of his fae magic. That's when he felt the warm, almost burning sensation in his gut and he felt the dread as a low red hue overtook him and Snow and before long he felt himself being hurled through a tunnel that he could only assume was some sort of transport magic like what Ethan used. The last thing he heard was Annalise's screams as he disappeared.

CHAPTER SIXTEEN

Annalise ran to Lachlan just as he disappeared, not just Lachlan but that woman, Snow as well. Annalise screamed, and fell to her knees, her face covered by her hands. He was gone, the love of her life and fiancé. Annalise looked around for any sign that Lachlan was still alive, but all she found was a lone black and white feather from his wings. Annalise held it close to her heart and left the fairy pools and her love.

A month passed and there was a funeral after it was apparent that Lachlan was indeed not coming home. The authorities searched for him and the woman Snow, but they found nothing, and Annalise knew they wouldn't. Some sort of strange light had taken Lachlan away, and there hadn't been a trace of him besides the feather she found. She couldn't very well tell anyone that Lachlan had sprouted wings. They already probably thought she was crazy, they hadn't said. Cassie Lachlan's mother seemed too, as had Kieran. They seemed more like the type that believed, and so Annalise had told them about the strange light and Lachlan's disappearance with Snow.

Annalise clutched the feather that had once been a part of

Lachlan's wing and closed her eyes tightly, wishing that she could see him again. She felt warm, very warm and when she opened her eyes, she saw she was engulfed in that strange light Lachlan and Snow had been. Then she was yanked from her bed and hurled through a tunnel. Annalise closed her eyes tightly, trying not to get sick as her stomach went flip-flop.

Annalise was finally hurled onto the grass outside Dunvegan castle, naked and cold. She tried to stand but stumbled instead and found she couldn't find her footing. Dizzy and disoriented, Annalise looked around. There was really nothing besides the castle behind her, and Annalise wasn't sure at that moment was real.

Annalise froze. "Lachlan?" She knew that voice, and it simply couldn't be. The love of her life was alive?

Around the corner of the castle came Lachlan Macleod, except he wasn't her Lachlan. No, this man was all wild and not as tame. His long black hair was curly and hung in ringlets down his shoulders. His heavy muscles showed in an outline under his tunic and his kilt all left nothing of the knowledge Annalise had that there would be nothing underneath.

He found her naked outside his castle, all woman and displayed for the damn world to see. He didn't know why that upset him. Perhaps she was one of Kieran's lasses? A part of him growled and was displeased. She was a beauty, but it wouldn't do for her to stay outside and freeze. She needed proper clothing and a warm bath. With that thought took off his tunic and handed it to the woman and she quickly put it on. She looked him up and down studying him and she came forward and touched the tattoos on his arms and Celtic wings on his back before nearly barreling him over with her hug.

"You are my Lachlan."

Lachlan couldn't bear to get her off of him but then he didn't have to for Cassandra, his mother and Lady of Dunvegan Castle, came over to him and helped the woman away from Lachlan and rushed her into the castle.

Lachlan sighed in relief, but remorse as well, and uncomfortable with the arousal he was experiencing. Something about that woman gave him warm and fuzzy feelings all over, and just now, when she held him, it felt right.

Annalise fought Cassandra the whole way into the castle and her room. The woman was a patient one, and Annalise had to hand it to her for that as she kept nagging the poor woman to see Lachlan again. Cassandra never spoke and only gestured to a wardrobe where she got out a dress and shoes. She motioned for Annalise to put on the dress, and she did glad that she had something more modest to wear.

"When will I get to see Lachlan?"

Cassandra just pointed at her and herself, walking in and eating. Annalise put a hand to her belly, which growled. It was likely lunchtime and she realized she hadn't eaten before being sucked into the same vortex that Lachlan of her... Period? Her time? She was clearly in another time, but what she was certain of was that she was definitely in Scotland. She was inside a room at Dunvegan Castle.

Annalise followed Cassandra out of the room and into the dining hall. Cassandra motioned for Annalise to sit beside Lachlan, Annalise's heart leapt in happiness and emotion when she saw him.

"Why did you leave?" Annalise asked him.

"What are you on about, lass? I am right here and have been my entire life."

Annalise shook her head. "You disappeared, and we had a funeral for you. "

Lachlan spit out the drink he had taken a sip of and stared at Annalise.

" I don't know if you are addled, but those are dangerous words."

" I am not crazy, you were gone and Snow was the reason you left."

Lachlan frowned. "How do you know my fiancé?"

" Fiancé!" Annalise exclaimed. "She is not your fiancé, I am." Annalise showed the ring he'd given her.

Lachlan stared at the ring and noticed the Macleod crest upon it. How could she have his ring, and he not know that she was to be his wife and not the woman now? Unless she was a dark magic user called a Vaith. If that was the case, then she would need to be watched. Until then, he would need to take care of her. Lachlan nodded at his brother Ethan, who had just walked in letting him know that this woman needed to be removed.

"From where do you hail?" Lachlan asked. "Your accent is English, are you from England?"

Annalise shook her head. "I moved to Scotland from Seattle in America."

Lachlan frowned. "The new world. Strange that you would come back to a country that is in war with England. Surely you knew that."

"I live on the isle of Skye, but my family hails from Ireland and parts of Scotland."

Lachlan nodded having heard enough and didn't bat an eye when his soldiers came and collected Annalise.

"What are you doing?" Annaliese exclaimed.

His mother frowned and gestured at him wildly.

"I cannot in good conscience keep a Vaith at my dinner table," Lachlan said.

"My name is Annalise O'Callaghan and you are my fiancé. You proposed to me and now you are arresting me?"

"I don't care Annalise. Until you have proven yourself,

you will be locked away," Lachlan said taking a drink of his alcohol.

He threw her into a room fit for a lady of the house and locked the door. Annalise screamed and banged on the door.

"Let me out, Lachlan!" Annalise sobbed. "Please." She slid down to land on her bottom where she grabbed her knees and held them as she cried.

"Please Lachlan; I love you." She said, her heart felt like it was breaking in two. "Please remember me."

CHAPTER SEVENTEEN

Cassandra's hands and body flew wild, and Lachlan only shook his head at her gestures.

"Don't have a go at me, Mother. I have a duty to protect my clan and if she is a Vaith, I am not taking a chance. She speaks of things that are clearly of another world, and you know what the elders might do to us if she is found to be a Vaith."

Cassandra motioned her gestures for food and drink.

"Don't fash, she will get her food. I am not cruel to let her starve."

Cassandra pointed at her ass, and Lachlan chuckled.

"Yes, I am an ass. She will eat and rest tonight, and tomorrow I will arrange for the test of the day. We will have our insurance, his mother. Cassandra shook her head and stand but I am sorry, I must do this. If you don't like it, go to your sisters I am sorry, I must do this. If you don't like it, go to your sisters.

Cassandra went to Annalise and even though she didn't know the other woman, she counseled her the best way she knew how. Annalise poured out every emotion to her and let all the pain go. She was fine later, and Cassandra motioned to the food the guards brought in. Annalise grabbed a tray and eat.

"Why don't you talk, Cassandra?".

Cassandra sighed and patted her throat and tried to talk, but only a weird sound came out.

"Oh, you cannot talk," Annalise said, and Cassandra appreciated Annalise caught on quickly.

Cassandra smiled at Annalise and gesture to the fire and in the wash basin and rubbed her arms. She was asking if Annalise wanted a bath.

"Yes, please!" Annalise said and Cassandra jumped up and walked out of the room and before too long the guards brought in a tub and some hot water and filled it.

When they were gone, Cassandra motioned for Annalise to get in and left the room. Annalise quickly got out of her clothing and jumped into the tub with a sigh. It felt so good and warmed the cold from her bones and lifted her spirits somewhat. She cleaned herself, and contemplated how she would get Lachlan to remember her, and find out what time period she was in. Judging by the tub and the way they filled the tub, she assumed medieval Scotland.

Lachlan muttered as he walked to the room he had Annalise thrown into. He should've gotten that damn ring from her and he hadn't. This was going to be hell. It was already bad enough she might be a Vaith, but damn it to all hell, she was talking openly of time travel and his death!? Anyone could have heard that. He unlocked the door and walked in.

"I must come for that ring and you will be handed over to me last and dash-" Lachlan stopped mid-sentence and just stared at Annalise in the tub, her eyes closed.

Lachlan swallowed adjusted himself and looked around the room and found the ring on the table close to the door he grabbed it quickly and left without Annalise knowing the wiser.

Annalise opened her eyes and smiled. She could hear his muttering just as she could when they were home. She had come up with a plan of slow torture giving up the ring he had given her. He would remember, come hell or high-water.

Lachlan slammed the door to his chamber and laid on his bed and stared at the ring he had supposedly given to Annalise. A memory flashed in his mind and Lachlan closed his eyes and grabbed his head. He could see Annalise splayed out for only his eyes to see. She moaned as Lachlan played with her clit, and when she came Lachlan was brought back to the present and the memory faded. What the hell was that? Lachlan shook his head and lifted his kilt and grabbed himself and began to rub. He pictured Annalise in the tub and the memory of her naked merged with it. He could see her in the tub as he played with her, he had no doubts that she would feel so good entering her. He knew exactly how he would pleasure her. She would scream his name as she came. If she weren't a Vaith then he could use her as a consort and take his pleasure with her. No harm would come to her as long as she lived in the castle. Was he an arse for thinking of doing as such with her? He was betrothed, but gods he needed, no wanted Annalise.

He would have her especially now that he knew that he had a memory of making love to her. Well, playing with her, but he was also sure that he had made love with her. It just felt right.

Snow was so excited about the idea of going to see Lachlan Macleod and finally having the Dunvegan Castle to herself as a lady of the castle. She could use her newfound power and bring down Lachlan once and for all and wipe out the Macleod clan. The MacDonalds would reign supreme and Dunvegan would be theirs for the taking. She would then move on to rule over Scotland and soon England. She would take back her role as a queen, and those pesky Tuatha dé Danann would be out of her and her sister's lives once and for all.

Snow cackled as she stared at herself in the mirror and waved a hand and the mirror swirled with clouds and soon showed Lachlan Macleod on his bed, his penis in his hand as he pleasured himself. How charming, even now Lachlan was thinking of her. Too bad, that room and its castle will be hers soon and the famorians would experience their glorious return. She would be celebrated and loved for centuries to come. Snow touched Lachlan's image in the mirror.

"Soon love, you will be mine and everything you own as well."

CHAPTER EIGHTEEN

Lachlan found Annalise downstairs in the kitchen with his mother. When had he given permission for her to be a release from her room? The Vaith test hadn't even been administered and already she was loose within the castle. Damn his mother and those guards for letting her free.

"What are you both up too?" he growled at them.

Cassandra and Annalise looked at Lachlan. Annalise frowned at him.

"Last time I checked I was a free woman able to do as I please."

Lachlan towered over her. "Not in my castle."

Annalise looked at Cassandra. "Bold this one is, isn't he?"

Lachlan growled again. "Go back to your room, Annalise."

She narrowed her eyes. "Make me."

Lachlan raised his eyebrows at the command. "Fine."

He grabbed her by the waist and slung Annalise over one of his shoulders. Annalise squeaked and Lachlan turned to his mother.

"She is going back to her room and you will not be letting

her out this time. Do that and I will throw you into your room for the night."

With that said Lachlan carried Annalise out of the kitchen and upstairs, but instead of locking her back in her room he entered his own and flung her unto his bed.

"You can't treat me like this Lachlan!" Annalise huffed as she stood up from his bed.

Lachlan unbuckled his belt and folded it.

"You've been naughty today and so you must be punished. I'm sorry lass but I must," Lachlan said

Annalise stared at the belt and backed away. "You aren't doing a thing to me with that."

"Want to bet?" he said and went after her.

Annalise ran around the room and the door, but before she could open it and run out Lachlan already had her in his arms and back on the bed on her belly, her dress pushed up and bare ass showing for the whole world to see. Lachlan brought down the belt and it connected to her butt with a 'smack'.

Annalise gasped and tried not to cry out. She would not let him know just how bad she felt with every spanking, but what alarmed her more was just how much the spanking aroused her. Lachlan finished and threw the belt to the floor. He stared at his work. Her ass was red and he felt a little guilty causing her so much pain but he was the laird of Dunvegan Castle dammit! He must show that he could handle one wench.

He stared at the flesh between her legs and realized just how much the act of spanking her was turning him on. He flipped Annalise onto her back and bent down and pressed his lips to hers and rubbed his hand from her breast and down to her belly to the apex between her thighs. He flicked her clit with a finger and Annalise bucked her hips.

Lachlan inserted a finger into her canal and found that

she was wet and ready for him. Annalise moaned into his mouth and when he broke the kiss, she screamed out her pleasure as he fingered her. Lachlan removed his finger and his hand went to his kilt. He unwrapped it and let it fall to pool around his feet.

Annalise watched as his penis, erect and hard, bobbed, the tip glistening in the light. She'd almost forgotten just how Lachlan looked naked and just how much she missed making love with him and how much she missed him as well.

"I want you, Lachlan, please," Annalise said.

Lachlan growled. "Then you shall have me, lass."

He bent over and covered her with his body and entered her in one swift thrust. They gasped and moved in tandem with each other, Lachlan thrusting and Annalise bucking her hips to meet each of his thrusts. Annalise screamed out her pleasure as it built and exploded. Lachlan growled as he felt her canal clench his penis. He thrust harder, faster until he felt his own orgasm build and he spilled his seed within her. Flashes of her laughter and her running from him split through his mind as he came, and Lachlan shook his head as he collapsed onto the bed beside her.

Annalise turned onto her side to look at him. "Does this mean you remember me Lachlan?"

"Nay lass, I remember naught who you are, but you are a good tup," he told her.

Annalise smacked him and got out of bed and walked to the door, naked.

"Where are you going in such a state?" Lachlan demanded.

"Back to my room. Unless you remember who I am, there will be no more 'tupping' me," Annalise said as she slammed his chamber door behind her as she left.

Lachlan draped an arm over his face and let out a tremendous sigh. He'd just made a huge mistake, and he realized he would pay for it.

How could he have sex with her and not remember who she was? Something wasn't right, he seemed to be blocked by something or someone. Snow perhaps? She'd used some sort of magic to transport him back to this time, right? Annalise dressed when she entered her room and walked to her window and looked out of it. She had a view of the garden and Cassandra was there with the two men, one with a scar down his cheek and another who looked suspiciously like Kieran!

Annalise ran from her room and out to the garden. It wasn't possible. How in the hell was Kieran here?

"Kieran." Annalise called to him, and he looked at her with a strange look on his face.

"Aye?" he said hesitating and unsure.

"It's me, Annalise. I'm staying with Lachlan on Skye at the cabin. We had a funeral for him."

Kieran looked at the other man. "Ethan, you know anything about this, methinks she is crazed."

Ethan chuckled. "Perhaps a bit addled brother, I will escort the lady back to her room."

Cassandra noticed Annalise and gave her a worried look before they escorted her back into the castle. Annalise wanted to scream in frustration. How in the hell did no one not know who she was? Lachlan had forgotten her and now his brother had too!

Ethan walked with her into the castle but pulled her into a broom closet.

"Uh...This isn't my room," Annalise said.

"Haud yer wheesht lass, what I am about to tell you is important," Ethan told her.

"What do you want to tell me that's so important to be said in a broom closet?" Annalise asked him.

"Lachlan and Kieran are under a powerful spell lass. Llyr, our father, has worked hard to bring Lachlan back to the place of his birth. Unfortunately, Snow got to him first and Llyr has been working to keep her from him."

"And Kieran?" Annalise asked.

Ethan shook his head. "Mirror image spell. Merely astral projection. Kieran will only remember his time here as a dream. As he sleeps in your realm, he is alive in ours and awake. No memories of his time here or there. But Lachlan is flesh, he is here because of Snow but stays here because of Llyr."

"Just who is Llyr?"

"King of the fae and the Tuatha dé Danann. Honestly, have you never heard of the fae?"

"I have heard of them, but thought they were a myth," Annalise told him. "But they are real?"

Ethan nodded. "Lachlan and Kieran are Tuatha dé Danann, born and bred to be rulers. Gods among humans. You'd be wise to open your eyes to the creatures that inhabit this realm. Now heed my warning, stay clear of Lachlan for your sake unless you would like to be targeted by the fae."

CHAPTER NINETEEN

The fae? Creatures of this realm? She was always taught that fae and other creatures were myth, nothing more. But now, since Ethan had said something, she was seeing some slight differences among the people of the castle. A tail hidden under a dress here, and horns hidden under hair there. Glamour everywhere. When Annalise watched Lachlan, he seemed to almost have that ethereal air around him. His skin glowed and the tattoos on his back rippled when she could spy on him when he was shirtless.

Annalise found several people at the castle who were comfortable talking of the fae and the Tuatha dé Danann. But none were more forthcoming than Lunasa, an elderly woman with blue spiral tattoos on her face and neck, disappearing into her tunic. She was a wealth of information and proved to be a superb hostess when she invited Annalise to her cottage in the village.

"Why does everyone hide their forms?" Annalise asked her.

Lunasa thought for a moment, as old women did when they were finding the right words to say.

"There are those who wish to profit or destroy the fae and Tuatha dé Danann."

"Why?"

"Why not? Wouldn't you like to have the tail of a dragon or the flesh of a fae for your illness?"

Annalise scrunched her nose in disgust. "This place isn't safe for them, why haven't they left?" Annalise asked. "The stories I have heard about the fae and Tuatha dé Danann all say they went underground and that all the fae folk had their own realms."

Lunasa laughed. "That's what they would like you to believe lass, the glamour helps them all blend in so they can live among us. Only the few with the sight can see them."

"Like me," Annalise said.

Lunasa nodded. "Like you."

Lachlan looked everywhere for Annalise. The gardens, kitchen, and her room. The wench was not to be found. He growled and sent for his horse. She had to have left the castle. He rode into the nearby village and didn't have to go far when he saw Annalise walking on her way back to the castle. Lachlan steered the horse toward her and kicked into a trot.

"Why are you out here? You are to stay at the castle," Lachlan told her.

"Now I can't visit my friends? You are proving to be an ass, Lachlan," Annalise said.

Lachlan halted his horse and offered his hand to her. Annalise took it and she was swung up onto the horse in front of him.

"I am an arse to be sure," Lachlan agreed. "But I am only protecting you, lass."

"Protected? I am not even protected from you, Lachlan. You said yourself that there will be a trial. A Vaith trial, you said. You expect to try me as a bad magic user. Isn't that a threat?" Annalise explained.

Lachlan said nothing as they rode back to the castle. Once back, Annalise slid from the horse and left Lachlan standing in front of the castle. Lachlan walked his horse into the stall and unhooked it from the saddle. He thought hard about what Annalise had said. It was indeed a threat to request Annalise be put on trial. Was he no better than those people who prosecute witches? He was Tuatha dé Danann, and he surely would know if she were a bad magic user. He would have to speak to his brothers and father about this.

Lachlan walked into the castle to find a surprise awaiting him. Snow, his fiancé had arrived. He walked over to her and her entourage. He took her hand and gave it a kiss, all the while staring at Annalise who shook her head, spun on her heel and ran from the room.

"M'lady, how was your travel here?" Lachlan asked her as Snow took his arm and they walked.

The men in her entourage followed close behind. She waived them off until one man remained. He was tall, had green eyes and an air of sophistication. He was a royal or part of the court, but something about him had Lachlan fearing for the worst. He was worried about Annalise.

Annalise flew into her room and fell onto her bed in a heap of sobs. She thought she could be strong, but she couldn't. Seeing Lachlan with Snow pierced through her heart like a spear. Lachlan wasn't lying when he'd said that Snow was his fiancé here in this time. She looked at the hand where the ring he had given her had been. What cruel god or goddess would take her fiancé away and then make him be in love with another woman in a different time? This wasn't fair and Annalise couldn't help but feel like something more was going on with Snow, as something was going on with Llyr, and Ethan. Annalise wiped her face and looked around her room. She got up and threw things around the room, screaming and letting out whatever anger and sorrow she had.

Kieran heard the screaming and breaking of glass and quickly ran to Annalise's room and found the lass trashing the whole place! He ran into the room and grabbed Annalise. She punched and struggled against him, but he only pulled her to his chest and soothed her. After a moment, Annalise collapsed with a sob.

"It's not fair," She kept repeating. "It's not fair."

Kieran tried to piece together what the lass was saying and then saw Lachlan and Snow coming into the room and then realized why. The lass was in love with his brother and he now had his fiancé here. Kieran smoothed out Annalise's hair and escorted the woman from the room in search of Cassandra. She was more equipped to handle this mess. He'd have some choice words with Lachlan when he saw him again and try to find out what his arse of a brother did to Annalise.

Later that night, Kieran found Lachlan in his room. Kieran closed the door behind him as he entered.

"What was that?" he asked his brother.

"That was the anger of a Vaith," Lachlan said.

Kieran frowned. "Not a Vaith, you know she isn't. You tupped her, didn't you?"

Lachlan flinched, and Kieran nodded.

"So you tup her and just throw her away. The lass obviously loves you and we both know you don't love this Snow woman. You showed such apprehension at having to be her fiancé, so why choose her now?" Kieran asked.

Lachlan flinched again at the word 'love'. "How was I to know that Annalise was in love with me? We only tupped once."

Kieran shook his head. "You told me, father, and Ethan

that she spoke of another time where you were her fiancé and that you died. You also said that you've been seeing one fate three every time she is near. We know that to see a fate means that Danu is giving you the gift of a future child, and that child is likely with Annalise."

"We don't know that for sure. Danu has her ways of doing things. It could be as simple as the fate coming to warn me about the lass."

Kieran chuckled. "Why lie to yourself, brother? The child's fate is yours, should you choose to accept it. I for one will not sit around and watch Annalise waste away from a broken heart. Woo both women, pick the one your heart most desires and not the one your cock wants more."

CHAPTER TWENTY

Annalise spent part of the night with Cassandra being loved on just like her own mother would do. Annalise thought of her mother then. She'd been beautiful and caring. To a fault, as years later when she'd let her sister move in, she was murdered. The suspect was her own sister, and for good reason, Annalise's aunt had disappeared that same night.

Would her mother have stayed nice and been the mother Cassandra was? She then thought of Lachlan and wondered if he'd make a great father. Shed hoped Lachlan would be by to check on her. She had torn her room in her despair. But he had been scarce the rest of the night though, and Annalise worried he was with Snow. The other woman must have planned this from the start. There was no way she didn't know Lachlan. She had specifically called him out back in their time where they'd fought.

Annalise snuggled in and closed her eyes. The sound of the door opening had her up and alert a few moments later. Annalise grabbed the small dagger called a sgian dubh. She climbed out of the bed and walked around her room and nearly yelled when she came face to face with Snow. The other woman glowed pale in the darkness and her eyes shone yellow in the night.

"Um...can I help you?" Annalise asked her.

Annalise was blasted into a wall, and she struggled to breathe as Snow appeared before her, laughing.

"How convenient that you'd be alone tonight, oh that's right, you are the lover of Lachlan. Well, once lover."

Annalise tried to stay conscious but was fading fast. Snow laughed again.

"How can a puny human be the lover and mate of a Tuatha dé Danann?"

Annalise lost consciousness then and the last thing she heard was Snows screams of outrage.

Lachlan paced outside of his mother's room as the healer tended to Annalise.

Hard to believe that Snow had been a Vaith all along, and Annalise had been the victim. How had Annalise survive being blasted into a wall? She wasn't Tuatha dé Danann, his father had confided in him she wasn't, but Lachlan was convinced that she had to be some sort of fae. Only someone of their realm could've survived that blast. The healer came out of the room and gave him a nod that he may now enter the room. Lachlan ran into the room and to Annalise's side.

" Och lass, you seem to be in some sort of trouble," Lachlan said as he pushed some of her hair from her face. She'd likely be out the rest of the night and into the wee hours of the morning. Lachlan bent over and kissed Annalise on her forehead and touched her soft lips with his own as well. Annalise stirred a moment and seemed distressed, but her brow eased and she went back into whatever peace she was in.

Lachlan walked out of the room and nodded to Ethan and Kieran, signaling them to follow him. They fell into step on either side of him.

"Find out where Snow is and bring her back here to be tested. Once we have a confirmation, then we can proceed with her sentencing," Lachlan barked.

Ethan and Kieran walked ahead, and Lachlan strode into his own room. He went to his wardrobe and pulled out his claymore. He would have to ride out to the MacDonald's, and demand they apologize for Snow's actions on Annalise.

Lachlan met with his mother and told of the situation at hand. Cassandra seemed concerned and frankly a little more anxious then Lachlan would have liked. His mother was getting older and her body frailer, he must remember to tell her of things gently.

"I'll leave in the morning, hopefully Annalise will still be asleep. The lass has a penchant for getting herself into trouble," Lachlan told Cassandra.

Cassandra signed to him. "Is it worth going to the MacDonald's? Perhaps she isn't associated with them?"

"She bears their clan mark, Mother. I cannot in good conscience allow a woman being attacked in my castle by a Vaith," Lachlan explained

Cassandra looked worried but nodded.

"Do what you must," she said, her voice harsh as she spoke to her son for the first time.

Lachlan lay in bed unable to sleep, his mother's harsh voice rippling through his mind and the image of Annalise laying there injured had him wide awake. He hadn't thought of what would happen when he confronted the MacDonalds. Was he to attack them or call them out? Lachlan growled and pushed the heels of his hands into his eyes. He flung his arms down to the bed and closed his eyes and pretended to be asleep. Soon, he was asleep and all thoughts of Annalise being injured seemed to disappear with a purple-haired child of the fates.

Morning, not something Lachlan was looking forward to.

He hadn't wanted to go to the MacDonald's, yet here he was riding with a small group of men to their ancestral home over one of their own attacking Annalise within Dunvegan. He didn't have to protect Annalise, there were no rules about this, but Lachlan felt duty bound to protect the woman. She, after all, had been his lover and talk around the castle had come to a brutal head when one maid had been found whispering that Annalise suffered a broken heart because she missed his bed. No, she had suffered a broken heart because Lachlan had been an idiot and an arse and had only been interested in doing as his dick had wanted. After a few miles, Lachlan called for them to stop for the moment and rest. He felt the dread in his stomach when he thought of the duty that was before him. This could either mean life or death, war or peace. Whichever way it fell to would make it difficult on his clan and likely cause their downfall.

CHAPTER TWENTY-ONE

Annalise woke a few days later, groggy and hurting badly. She tried to move but found she couldn't as she felt like her body was jello all over. Annalise groaned and tried to remember what happened. It all came flooding back in a giant wave. Snow had come to her room and attacked her, blasted her into a wall. God, she hurt badly. She worked through the pain and looked around her room. In the corner Cassandra sat with her eyes closed and Annalise whimpered, which had the mother of the Laird of Dunvegan jumping from her seat and to her side.

Cassandra fussed over her and didn't let Annalise tack at all for a good moment, and when she got to speak, she only got a sentence out.

"Where is Lachlan?" she asked.

Cassandra said nothing for a long moment and then finally opened her mouth to speak.

"He went to the MacDonald's to fight."

Annalise stared at the woman, shocked to actually hear her speak instead of gesturing with her hands. She spoke surprisingly well for a woman without a tongue.

"When will he be back?"

Cassandra signed 'days.'

Annalise understood, they weren't in their own time where there were cars. They had carriages and horses here. It would likely take him longer than normal to get there and get back to the castle. Annalise only hoped that he didn't start a war with the other clan defending her.

Lachlan made perfect time to the castle of the MacDonald's. They weren't too open to them, but the laird allowed them audience.

"I am here because one of your own attacked a lass and threw her into a wall. I seek retribution due to these events and humbly request she be punished. She goes by Snow," Lachlan addressed the laird.

The MacDonald laird just stared at him for a moment before speaking. "We do not have such a woman within our clan. Are you certain she was a MacDonald?"

"She claimed as such and came with a sizable dowry for her hand in marriage."

The laird shook his head. "No, no one by that name. My daughter is no more than three and my oldest girl died last summer."

"My condolences to you, my laird," Lachlan told him.

The laird nodded and looked around his audience chamber. He pursed his lips as he gazed upon his clan and wondered who this Snow was and why she had told Laird Macleod that she hailed from the MacDonald? This was odd indeed. They had a feud with Macleod but this was topping that. Now they were accused of having a daughter of MacDonald attacking one of the Macleod's and that simply couldn't go without some sort of punishment. If he found out who this woman was, he would make a fine example of her for her lies and treachery.

Lachlan left that afternoon back to his camp and

wondered if the MacDonald laird was indeed speaking the truth. He seemed to be, but then again, he was a MacDonald.

"He is at the MacDonald's, my lady"

"So he is. Unfortunately, he won't get far. I only pretended to be part of the clan," Snow said. "But I thank you Joseph, you have been very valuable to me."

Joseph beamed at the compliment and bowed low. Snow waved him away and went back to her scrying. There she saw the child, one of the fates three helping Lachlan and the bitch Annalise. Danu apparently had her hand in all of this, meddlesome goddess. Snow wished there were a way to get the goddess taken care of. Unfortunately, no other god or goddess, whether they were Tuatha dé Danann or not, would interfere with her work. Shit, she wasn't even Scottish and the goddess was in Scotland. It proved that even a goddess from Ireland could travel to Scotland and be welcome here.

Snow splashed her hand into the water to rid it of the image and realized that she may have to go to the drastic plan she had to ensure that Lachlan perished. She wanted all the Tuatha dé Danann but that seemed so unrealistic right now. Snow went back to scrying, this time to look upon the MacDonald Laird, he was playing with his daughter and Snow had an awful but brilliant idea. This would be better than her original plan, and it would involve just a little trickery on her part. Snow laughed with true glee, and Joseph stared at her curious. She stopped and looked at him and motioned for him to come to her. He came willingly and Snow pressed her lips to his and fell back onto the bed pulling him on top of her.

Annalise kicked the horse into a gallop. She couldn't let Lachlan go by himself on her behalf. This was all insane; Lachlan was going to get himself killed. There was a feud still going on between the MacDonald and Macleod and Lachlan was going to talk to the laird of that clan! What was he, stupid?!

If she rode the horse hard, she would get to Lachlan faster. Cassandra had told her that he was likely on his way back by now. If she could meet him on the way back, she could talk to him about Snow. She had to get Lachlan to remember before it was too late. She didn't want there to be a war, but Snow had made it clear when she was attacked that there would be a war, and that Annalise would not be able to stop it. She could damn well try, and right now a war between the Macleod's and MacDonald's would not be a good thing.

She knew what time period she was in now, 1406!? And if she could remember anything from her time at university, it was her very Scottish teacher telling the class about the clan war between the Macleod's and MacDonald's. That they would win but at a terrible cost to their clansmen. That's when she realized that the fairy flag has been around her the whole time. That piece of cloth that was so sacred to its clan, Clan Macleod. Annalise put her horse into a trot, and then stopped to rest. This whole time she could have been looking for the fairy flag and trying to stop Snow. She wouldn't be here riding a horse to meet Lachlan and convince him not to mess with the MacDonald's and that something seemed wrong.

Annalise almost didn't hear the approaching riders, and she quickly found a spot in her small campsite to hide.

"A campsite?" a familiar voice said. "Whoever stayed here must be asked, friend or foe."

"Whoever stayed here is hiding." Lachlan's voice shouted,

"Come out or must I find ye and cut yer bowels from your body."

Annalise felt such a relief fall over her when she heard his voice, it meant she didn't have to be alone and that she'd made it. She came out of her hiding spot, and Lachlan and Kieran froze.

"Annalise...Lass, what are you doing out here?" Lachlan fumbled.

"I needed to come to warn you to not go to the MacDonald's. Nothing good comes out of it Lachlan. You went into a wolves' den and gave yourself to them when you have a feud with them. How stupid could you be?" Annalise scolded.

Lachlan smirked, his braw, wee lass lecturing him the Laird of Dunvegan and Clan Macleod. How much he loved her from the minute she'd stepped onto that plane. What was a plane? A memory flashed and showed himself proposing to Annalise and giving her the ring with his clan crest pressed inside it with a single scrawl of words 'Forever my love, to the stars and beyond'.

Lachlan felt different and when he looked around, he was confused. Where was he? Scotland, yes, his home. He looked at Annalise and then he smiled at her and the world seemed less complicated. She was here and so was he, and that's all that seemed to matter in the world at that moment.

"You are bold lass, I like it," Lachlan told her, still reeling from the memory.

"Yes, and you are still an ass," Annalise told him.

"A big one, it seems," Lachlan said with a laugh. "Come, let us go back to camp and rest. It's not far from here."

Annalise climbed onto her horse and followed Lachlan and Kieran to camp. Thirty minutes later, they rode into camp and Lachlan helped her off of her horse. He took her to a bigger tent in the middle of the camp, his tent.

"You can sleep here, and before you argue I suggest you

do as your told lass. I don't want to have to punish you again," Lachlan told her.

Annalise clenched, but not at the memory of the belt on her behind, but of the arousal she had when he'd done it. She felt the aching so badly that clenching was the only thing she could think of doing. Lachlan smirked at her and Annalise struggled to squash the feelings down but gave him a well-deserved smack on his shoulder. It was awkward, painfully so, but after a moment Lachlan left her alone to do rounds with his men. Annalise climbed onto Lachlan's cot and closed her eyes and let exhaustion pull her into sleep.

The next morning Annalise woke up to birds singing and the sound of a waterfall? Annalise bolted upright and found Lachlan smiling at her.

"Mornin' lass," he told her

Annalise looked around and said. "Where are we?"

Lachlan looked at the fairy pool beyond. "This is where I proposed to you. I remember that, Annalise."

Annalise felt her heart race and jumped up and crushed her lips onto Lachlan's and knocked him to the ground. She straddled him and Lachlan moaned into her mouth. He lifted her dress and moved back a bit of his kilt and entered her. Annalise moaned and rode him until their bodies glistened in the morning sun.

Annalise lay with Lachlan and traced lazy circles around one of his nipples, making it into a hard nub. Lachlan sighed and pulled her closer into his armpit. Annalise was so happy to know that Lachlan remembered their proposal and that she was his fiancé and not Snow. But why did she suddenly pity the woman? She had been mean in their time, and scary. Annalise had to look into this and find out more about Snow before she could say anything to Lachlan about her. Perhaps she was just a woman whose power became too much? That was a great question, Annalise added that to her brain file for the book she was still writing.

"Lachlan, do you remember anything else? Your mom and dad, brother and sister?"

"No, I know I have two brothers and no sister. I don't know another mom like I do with Cassandra and the only dad I have known is Llyr."

There was that name again! Who was Llyr? Ethan had said one of the Tuatha dé Danann but Annalise knew nothing about them and felt that she should.

"Llyr?"

"High king of the Unseelie and my father," Lachlan explained.

"High king! You're a prince?!"

Lachlan chuckled. "Only in the Otherworld. Here in Scotland, I am only known as Laird of Dunvegan and Clan Macleod."

"The Otherworld?"

"Aye, it is a place of untold beauty where the fae, Tuatha dé Danann and other creatures can go to live, though most of us would rather live in this plane of existence. A place where we are tolerated."

"But not accepted," Annalise said.

She felt Lachlan nod, and Annalise closed her eyes in thought and said, "Let's get them to come to our modern time. Surely they'd be accepted there."

Lachlan looked down at her and frowned. "As guardian of the door to that time and plane of existence I can only say no, it would not be wise to open the door and let those of the Otherworld there. I know they'd likely be accepted given Halloween and cosplay.

"How do you know about cosplay and Halloween?"

"Samhain first and I don't know how I can remember cosplay." Lachlan laughed. "It's strange I can remember that but not of the family you told me I have in the other time. I feel guilty that I cannot remember and that maybe I am not the son they saw me as."

"It's alright Lachlan, we can get through this together and if you still struggle with your memory we can have it looked at in the other time and see a doctor."

"I don't think it's that drastic and they wouldn't know what to do. This is a spell and a very powerful one at that," Lachlan said

Annalise nodded, it was indeed and whoever cast it meant business.

Lachlan zipped them back to camp where they ate a bit of meat and cheese before they pressed on their way back to Dunvegan castle. It was hard to believe that he now was remembering her and that Llyr's spell was breaking. His own father had been the reason he was under that spell as Ethan said, but now Annalise felt confident that she had finally broken it and that Snow was now in the wind never to return. She wanted to go home with Lachlan and back to their lives in their own time, but that was likely not going to happen as she was beginning to realize that they were stuck in this time and that Lachlan and no other being like him could possibly send them both home.

Annalise and Lachlan holed up in the Laird's quarters and made love and slept once they got back to Dunvegan Castle. No one talked to them, no one dared to say a thing about the change in the relationship between their laird and Annalise. They somehow knew something was going on and they weren't about to add to it. As far as they were concerned, Annalise was now the new fiancé, the soon to be lady of Dunvegan, as Lachlan had announced when they had entered the castle, much to Annalise's shock. She looked forward to being back with Lachlan, but she was not sure she was ready to be a lady over a giant castle. On the other hand, everyone seemed to be in a good mood and the gloom that was part of the castle when Snow had come seemed to have lifted and now sunshine was filtering into the rooms, flowers being set out and the women tittered with happiness.

She was truly happy, and she supposed she could stay in this time period and live out the rest of her life with Lachlan without technology or running water. It was a trade she had been willing to make when she had started on her mission to get Lachlan to remember her. Was she wrong for it? Another woman had been pushed aside and now forgotten like she never existed in the castle. Annalise felt a little saddened for Snow; the other woman had only been looking for love and when she had attacked Lachlan in their time, she had said that she wanted him for her own. She wasn't going to feel bad, Lachlan hadn't known her then and barely knew her now, she was going to enjoy and bask in Lachlan's love and the coming festivities. Christmas was on the horizon and Lachlan had ordered the castle be decorated for the special occasion.

He wanted everything to be lovely for Annalise, everything he did for now on was going to be for her, he promised her. He'd apologized too, for what? Annalise didn't think she knew. Annalise looked down at her hand and the Macleod crested ring that rested on her engagement finger. Lachlan had put it back on her finger at the Fairy Pools and made sure she knew that she was his and his only. Yes, Annalise was truly happy, and she was ready to live her life just like this and for once she accepted that all men weren't the same. Lachlan sure wasn't Joseph Declan and Annalise realized just how far she had come from that scared little woman running from Seattle to Scotland. Living here had made her stronger and she no longer worried about what would happen with Joseph Declan and truth be told, if she ever faced him again, she knew she could handle him herself.

CHAPTER TWENTY-TWO

She walked around the garden and watered the plants that Cassandra had designated to her to care for. She was happy to help in this wonderful place, but what happened in the drawing room with Lachlan and the talk they had before lunch had Annalise thinking why he wanted to go back to the place she was found. Was he searching for the feather that she had lost? Or searching for some other way to send her home? She hoped not, she was able to care for herself and because of that, she was going to stay here in 1490 and that was that. He would have to send her away kicking and screaming, and find someone that would keep her in the modern time because, without a doubt, she would find a way back to Dunvegan in this time again.

Annalise looked at Cassandra who stood before the rose bush, so still. She thought it strange that she wasn't moving, just staring straight ahead at the bush. Annalise stood, and walked over to her and grabbed her on her shoulder and when she turned Cassandra to face her, she crumpled into her arms her face a mask of pain and tears as she heard the crack of a gun in the air. A bullet pierced her breast, and

Annalise tried to put pressure on it, but Cassandra shook her head. She gestured to Annalise but she couldn't understand. Cassandra tried to whisper to her, but nothing came out as she struggled to talk and then took one last breath and was gone. Annalise screamed for help, and it seemed like it was forever that help finally did come, and when Lachlan came, Annalise couldn't bear to see the anguish on his face seeing his mother dead in her arms.

They buried Cassandra a day later, Lachlan hadn't wanted to wait for a wake for her, he wanted her burial swift and quick. It was just as he'd been raised, Cassandra had expressed in her writings that she didn't want to be mourned and wanted to be buried among the flowers in the garden.

Annalise watched as another important woman in her life was buried. She had lost three now, her mother, Cassandra, and Lunasa had left her. Lunasa to the village who had pushed her out finally and she had to move on. That day hadn't been near as sad as losing Lady Cassandra. Annalise covered her mouth and nose with her hand, and let the tears flow as Lachlan's arms went around her and his plaid wrapped around her to keep the winter cold out and keep her warm.

Annalise leaned into his embrace and allowed the sound of his beating heart to calm her. She felt him kiss her on top of her head and said with a steady voice, "I love you Annalise."

"I love you too, Lachlan," Annalise said and his arms tightened around her as they both watched Cassandra's body being lowered into the grave at the base of the flower garden.

"Good bye, Cassandra. May we see you again," Annalise whispered to the evening air.

A week later, Lachlan and Annalise had that garden shining, potted flowers, plants, trees and every kind of vine they could think of. Even Llyr helped with the garden for his late wife. Perhaps he felt guilty for not attending her funeral? Annalise turned her attention back to Lachlan who was talking to Nathaniel and Ethan. They all were hunched over, and it was apparent that it was a huddle among brothers and not friends. Ethan looked at Annalise then, and she wondered what it was they were talking about. Annalise took a sip of her drink in honor of Cassandra's garden, and tried not to look back at him. Something about that gaze had her uncomfortable.

Lachlan found Annalise and took her aside later that night, and he escorted her back to the castle and their room. Once there Lachlan begins to undress her slowly as he pushed her towards their bed, kissing Annalise's neck and lips feverishly. There was a burn building between her legs, she needed him, needed him like she needed a drink. He undressed showing off the muscle, and six pack abs going down into a happy trail of muscle. This was a tall drink of water. Annalise reached out her hands and let her fingers trace down his chest and downward to his penis and gripped it in her hand. Lachlan shuddered and groaned, and Annalise heard him whisper her name. She rubbed him for a good while and she finally had enough, she shed off the dress and presented her ass in the air for him like a dog in heat. Lachlan laughed behind her but obliged and before she could react, he was inside her with a hard thrust. Annalise screamed out and fell forward gripping the blankets as he pulled out slowly and entered her again with a hard thrust. He kept up the pace a few more times and finally began to make love to her from behind.

They lay in each other's arms, and stared up at the castle ceiling, wishing they could both be outside, naked under the stars. He turned to Annalise.

"What does your father do for work?"

"I thought I told you."

Lachlan shook his head and Annalise realized she hadn't told him about Dad's job.

"I am sorry, Dad's line of work is that of mercenaries and artifacts and science," she told him. "In fact, he has an area under the mansion he deems to be his most prized possession which I think is just a tactic for thieves to come and steal it, only to be tricked and caught."

Lachlan looked doubtful, and even Annalise knew that seemed a little far-fetched. "I think it's just some artifact he found and doesn't want to share it."

Lachlan nodded at Annalise, and she changed the subject by pointing out the window. "Look, it's snowing again."

Annalise got up from the bed taking the blankets with her and ran to the window to watch the flurries fall.

CHAPTER TWENTY-THREE

A WEEK PASSED AND THEY WATCHED. WATCHED AND FOUND NO sign of movement, the MacDonald and Snow were not budging and if they were, they were likely engaged in their own problems. They would find out who'd killed lady Cassandra and why, Annalise stayed firm to her belief that Snow was the only one who could be the culprit behind the murder. The woman seemed hell bent on making Lachlan's life a living hell at this point in time. But one thing that bothered Annalise more was that before she attacked Lachlan in the modern time, she'd said that she loved him. It seemed wrong that she would say those words to Lachlan, like Snow knew him and couldn't divulge that. Now she could claim Lachlan if she wanted because he hadn't remembered Annalise. He was free for the taking.

She didn't blame Snow for that, but it did unfortunately bother her more than anything. It was more that she was jealous as well, because the other woman was obviously someone Lachlan knew at one time and then she realized that Lachlan in their time knew nothing of Snow. But she'd seen that face before, on the Skye Bridge, it had to be Snow who had knocked her in the Loch had the same features and the same hair and eyes. She had been flirting with Lachlan that day too, by batting her eyes at him. She hadn't meant to push Annalise off the bridge. She hadn't known that Annalise didn't know Lachlan as well then and she certainly wasn't in love with him at that time. Snow had traveled through time and must have gotten the dates they'd met mixed up. This was a major slip up for Snow, and now Annalise knew that Snow was not an innocent bystander in this mess. She was definitely instigating it all because she couldn't have Lachlan. That had to be the only reason.

Annalise went to Cassandra's grave and put some flowers on it, dusting the snow from the stone had been set. She sat down beside her, and opened her sheaf of parchment paper, and began to write and read out her words to Cassandra. She managed to get in several chapters of the book and wrote down some of her thoughts. She'd need to do more research and to include her time here. She wanted that for her character, to experience what she felt and smelled and heard in a Scotland vastly different from the modern. Here everything seemed fresh, and well cared for. The people of this Scotland took pride in living in this country, in the modern time she'd known some that weren't as happy that they were living in a great country with a proud history. She hoped to sway her readers whoever they may be, to go visit Scotland and her beauty.

Snow walked into the foyer of Clan MacDonald and snickered. How sad it was that this clan was so out of sorts. They scrambled like rats looking for a meal. Convincing the Laird of the clan wouldn't be so hard now that she'd taken what meant most to him. Snow bowed to the laird and put on a look of solemnity on her fair features.

"Oh great laird, I am so grieved to hear of your missing daughter," Snow told him.

"We never announced she was missing, who are you?" the MacDonald asked.

"I am Snow, you must remember me? I was the wench that you sent to Lachlan to wed him to patch the feud."

The MacDonald seemed to think for a moment before he accepted what she said without a fight.

"Fine, have you any news then?"

"No news, just that I think I may know who stole the wee lamb," Snow said

The Laird perked up at that and his men quickly cornered Snow. Snow laughed and looked at the laird.

"Do you think you can hurt me?" she taunted and the MacDonald bristled and then seemed to back off. It was not a good idea to provoke Snow.

The chief looked at his men and with a nod they backed away weapons gone.

"Tell me who has my daughter?"

Snow gave them the most beautiful smile. "Why the Macleods, don't you know? The feud you have had for so long and just when it's about to be patched up I come home and your daughter goes missing. Hardly a coincidence, don't you think?"

The laird frowned and the woman beside him gasped. This must be the girl's mother. No matter. She knew she would win.

"Oh aye, not a coincidence but of course what do I know, I am just a wench from this castle you handed over," Snow told him.

The laird nodded and looked around at his clan once more, and then to his wife he said, "We will find her even if we have to burn Dunvegan to the ground." He looked to his men. "We will attack every village on Skye until we take down the Macleods. I will have my daughter back!"

The men all huzzahed and Snow gave another small snicker. But that snicker died away when the woman who could only be the laird's wife seemed to look through her just as Annalise had. What is with these women who seemed to know what she was? She would have to rectify this situation, and she knew the best way. She'd have to make the lady of MacDonald clan disappear just like her daughter. Chaos, oh how Snow loved to play in it. It had been her job when she'd been a fates three, and not many fates who were reborn could remember their time as one.

Snow was lucky, she was reborn with all of her memories, that damn Danu and her brood of cauldron stirrers. They hadn't taken her seriously she'd meant that she would stay with her memories, and be reborn. She'd told them she wouldn't be forgotten. She was meant to be his mate, only his for all eternity, but unfortunately her rebirth had been to a stillborn and then later skipped and she became Snow. She'd lived in a wonderful castle with royal parentage, but over the centuries her kingdom was getting suspicious of her beauty and everlasting youth. So, Snow left and never looked back. She would not be forgotten, and Lachlan would be hers as he should be.

Lachlan found Annalise in the library reading through a giant tome. He hadn't known they'd had a book that huge! Must have rubbed the writer's hand raw. He shook his head and went to her and she looked up from her book and gave him a small smile.

"How fairs the writing today, lass?" he asked her as he moved her hair from her face.

"I am researching today, I feel like I haven't done this book justice, and I want to be known for accuracy and the right things," Annalise rambled and then she realized that Lachlan remembered her book. "Do you remember the iPad you gave me and how angry I was that you thought I was a charity case?"

"Aye, I do. I remember you cussed me out so bad that you had me nearly backed with fear. I thought you'd hit me for that."

Annalise's eyes spilled with tears, and she jumped into Lachlan's waiting arms. He twirled her around and around and gave her a passionate kiss.

"I remember everything lass, absolutely positively every wee thing," he laughed joyfully.

Annalise couldn't have counted her blessings at that moment! Her plan had worked, and Lachlan had returned to her, but why did she feel saddened that the Lachlan from this time period could never come back? She'd begun to love that side of Lachlan and hoped that at least a fragment of who he was here in this time period remained. Lachlan laughed once more, and Annalise delighted in seeing that handsome face so happy despite the gloom that had fallen over them all since Cassandra's death.

The MacDonald chief looked so aggrieved and Snow couldn't help but feel such glee from it all. Now his wife had gone missing thanks to Joseph Declan, who knew that human male was capable of doing this all? He delighted in hurting others and did it so well that Snow had even begun to feel nervous around him as well when she'd told him to carry out her dirty deeds.

The MacDonald looked to Snow for guidance. and she pleaded with all of his sensibilities and put the Macleods to the forefront of his mind time and time again. Gently reminding him that the Macleods were to blame for the disappearances and that action should be taken. He finally ordered some of his clansmen go out and scout out the Macleods for signs of his daughter or wife. Snow hadn't counted on that. She realized that Joseph had the two girls far enough away that it was unlikely that Joseph and his pitiful human body could get the two to Dunvegan before the MacDonald's men got there. She could take a chance and teleport the girl at least to the castle but then she would be confronted with being seen and that was a problem. She would have to look into her scrying bowl and figure out what she could do by searching for answers within it. It was the only way to make sure that her plans weren't for naught.

Decorating continued as the mood lifted from the gloom, Annalise felt safe and warm for now despite all of the time spent mourning Cassandra. Cassandra would have wanted them all to move forward from her death heads held high with a sharp tongue. Lachlan, the last few days, seemed at peace but still mourning the loss of Cassandra. Annalise knew this because he would go out to her stone and sit with her at night. That's how she knew he was the Lachlan from this time period through and through. He'd always been that way and she never saw it because she was blind to it all. She hadn't known Lachlan for that long, but he'd already lived through centuries before he'd met her.

"When were you going to tell me you were from 1490?" Annalise asked him one day.

"I was going too, but then the weird things began to happen. Like the woman and then Snow. Nothing seemed to snap back to reality, the reality that I had built for myself," Lachlan explained. "I just didn't want you to think I was crazy, but I never thought I would be sent back in time, and I certainly didn't know that Snow would do that and that you'd become involved, that my own sire was involved."

Annalise nodded, she understood completely, having been with a man who had abused and used her for four years. She'd built a reality for herself two years into the engagement.

Lachlan smiled at her and looked out the window and seemed lost in thought again. It wasn't a thought, but a memory of that time so long ago when he'd been young. He'd met Snow when they had been children. She wasn't known as Snow then but as Cerridwyn, named after the goddess of knowledge (check this).

That's when he'd learned that she was his mate and they were to be wed when they were older to strengthen the bond. But tragedy struck, and Cerridwyn was slaughtered along with her family and most of their clan when they were on their way home. She came back as Snow somehow and ever since, Lachlan would find her following him, like she had on that day she followed him passed the door that he was to guard and into the modern world for the rest of his life. He'd confronted her as well and had tried to convince her that they weren't mates anymore, their love had gone away and that there was nothing they could do about it.

"Why can't you be mine?" she'd asked.

"You must move on, lass," Lachlan told her and Snow only back up a few steps with a shake of her head.

"No, we choose our own destinies. Will you join me

Lachlan? Let's go way from this place, far away to another realm. We could start a new there and have our family," Snow told him.

Lachlan shook his head. "My bond with my mate will be strong, and I cannot let it go. I have to find her."

Snow squeezed her eyes shut. "So, you'll go and find her even though you know it's not possible to find her?"

"I'll go because you too have a mate out there, and we cannot grieve for too long over things we have lost along the way," Lachlan told her before he'd left her there in that cemetery where her family had been buried.

Lachlan wished that he could tell Annalise that he'd known her and that their relationship had been one of a mate, and that because Annalise was now his mate, Snow was jealous. It's a sad truth that Snow had lost him the first go round and found him again the next. That's why she'd begun to torment him as much as she could. She hadn't counted on him finding his mate so soon and knowing on the spot that Annalise was for him. Still, he was surprised he had forgotten about Snow when he'd seen Annalise. Maybe that was due to Llyr's magic? He didn't know but he had forgotten her and if she knew that, he was certain Snow would only just act out on it all. She was still very much obsessed with him and wouldn't stop until either of them was dead.

CHAPTER TWENTY-FOUR

THE WEEK OF CHRISTMAS, ANNALISE WAS SURPRISED WITH A gift from Lachlan. It was a beautiful necklace which held a twinkling blue sapphire and a raven was carved into the metal surrounding it.

"An early gift for you my love," Lachlan told her and put the necklace around her neck.

Annalise was floored, never had she owned something so incredibly beautiful. She'd come from money, but she had never been fond of buying the most expensive things like her friends growing up had. No jewelry, no designer brand clothing or purses. But this, this necklace, with its sapphire and raven design had her gushing with pride, and for once she didn't feel the need to feel guilty for Snow.

Lachlan smiled at her. "Cassandra would have loved to see it on your neck. Sorry, I don't mean to bring up grim tidings when these are supposed to be tidings of joy and laughter."

"She would have loved it and would have approved as well."

Lachlan felt a little better about bringing up Cassandra,

and decided it was time that Annalise began to mingle. So, he took her arm in his and walked her around the big ballroom introducing her to the clan and basked in her laughter and voice as she told her stories or laughed at other's stories and jokes. Annalise was a natural, and his clan seemed to love her. Someone called for music to play, and Lachlan pulled Annalise onto the dance floor as the someone promptly began to play music.

"What are you doing?" Annalise asked Lachlan when he pulled her in close.

"Dancing, have you never danced before?" Lachlan said

"Not since Joseph, and with him it was always followed by a beating because I stepped on his toe or made the wrong move."

Lachlan tried to control the anger that welled up inside of him at the thought of his woman being beaten down by such a weakling of a man. Any man who raised a hand to a woman in violence was low in his opinion. The memory of Annalise's bare ass being spanked by his belt. His face heated and he tried to control the sudden erection brooding between his legs. Annalise looked at him.

"I think we best find a spot for the night," Lachlan growled in her ear. "There is something I have been meaning to do to you again." Annalise felt heated and the spot at the apex of her thighs melted.

"What's that?" she whispered back breathlessly

"Are you wanting to feel the belt on your ass right now lass?" he asked her.

Annalise shivered and that was all Lachlan needed and soon they were leaving the party and going upstairs to their bedroom. Lachlan kissed her up against the door and pulled up her dress until he could grasp her bare ass. He pushed open the door and backed her up to the bed. Lachlan left her for a second to close and lock the door and then moved back over to her. He lifted her dress once more and pushed her back onto the bed. He kissed her belly and trailed down between her thighs. Annalise bucked her hips as he began to suck on her sensitive nub. Annalise moaned and arched her back, his tongue slid from that nub and down to her opening. He pushed into it to get a taste of her and that nearly shattered him too soon. He had to be inside her now. Lachlan covered Annalise with his body and slammed into her.

Annalise arched her back and let out a scream as she felt him hard and deep inside her. Lachlan pulled out to the tip, and then slammed back into her. He thrust faster and stronger, he had Annalise moaning his name and screaming out her moans. Her voice reverberated off the stone walls and Lachlan came apart at the seams. He spilled his seed inside her just as Annalise requested he 'fuck' her. Lachlan felt himself grow hard again at that request, but this time he had her up on her feet and pulling off her dress until she sat naked in front of him.

Lachlan took himself in his fist and rubbed before he grabbed his belt and walked back over to her. Annalise got excited when she saw what he held and turned and raised her ass into the air.

"Do it," she said.

Lachlan smacked her lightly at first and messaged her cheek. He smacked her harder, and Annalise moaned. Lachlan smacked her one more time and entered her from behind. Annalise moaned at how deep he was, filling her up so completely. Lachlan moved in and out and set a rhythm as Annalise came with a loud moan. Lachlan thrust faster as he felt his own release building once more and he thrust into her one last time and let himself go.

They lay listening to the music playing outside as the party moved. Annalise lay her head onto Lachlan's chest and made lazy circles on his chest. She stopped for a moment and Lachlan kissed her on her head.

"What are you thinking?" Lachlan asked her.

"I was thinking about Snow. Why is she so consumed by you? Did you know her?"

Lachlan sighed. "Yes, I knew her. But not as you know her."

"Tell me about her."

Lachlan nodded and began his story. He told of a girl who was to be his mate, and how her family and his were so excited at the union. But while her family and her were out on vacation they were ambushed and killed.

"She must have found reincarnation and came back as Snow. She found me a month before we met on the plane in Seattle," Lachlan explained. "She'd been so distraught when she saw me, and we did try but there wasn't a bond and we knew it. I had to leave her, my mate was out there, and she wasn't the one."

Annalise swallowed. "Did you love her?"

"No, I didn't. It's not because she wasn't the one, but because of how desperate she was just to be with me. It scared me, truly and caused problems with us. I finally had her back with her family and then a month later the strange things began to happen."

"What kind of strange things?" Annalise asked.

"Your home burning down and the woman that attacked us." Lachlan shook his head. "It just screamed Snow. She is truly messed up in the head. Do you know the story of the Fates Three?"

"No."

Lachlan nodded and climbed out of bed and walked over to one of the bookshelves that was in his room. He pulled a book down and returned to bed.

"This book is given to all Tuatha dé Danann youth, it tells

our stories and about the fates. These aren't mere fates, they are three little children either girl or boy and they are the keepers of the thin line between their lives and to their destinies," Lachlan explained. "Each child will get to be reborn as a mortal child, destined to become a Tuatha dé Danann if they are born of one or a human child who will find its everlasting mate."

"Everlasting mate?"

Lachlan smiled. "There is a bond that everyone has with their lovers. Those in the Otherworld have that mate bond and are destined to find the person they are meant to be with for eternity. But death before the bond can attach, that changes the bond for a fate, once they die they are brought back and they are supposed to have a different mate. This is why Snow cannot accept this. Not all fates remember their time as a fate, but Snow does, I remember her stories when we were kids."

"Are they not supposed to share them?"

"She said that they are not normally supposed to even remember their time as a fate, that only a rarer few could remember but she didn't know what happened to them at all," Lachlan explained.

Annalise frowned. "Well if they are to be reborn, maybe they go back to where they originate and then come back when its time."

Lachlan shrugged. "It's a thought, but maybe she was lying as well. Snow was so desperate that she would say anything to get me to agree to stay with her."

Annalise nodded and brought her knees to her chest. "I have been feeling awful about helping you remember me. I feel like I stole you from her."

Lachlan looked at her. "You did, but not because you are a cuckold. You and I share the bond, we were meant to be with one another."

"Yes, but who is her bond mate?" Annalise asked.

"I don't know, no one truly knows who their mates are until they feel that bond as we felt that bond," Lachlan explained.

Annalise nodded. It was like a ball of electricity that sent warmth down a line. It was one of a kind, and so strong that she could feel Lachlan on the other end. But still, Snow being distraught, what if she didn't have a mate bond? What if she were doomed to be without that great love of her life, and Annalise, like before, felt for her, but after talking to Lachlan, Annalise was now at ease knowing that she hadn't hurt Snow, and that Snow's obsession was real and that she was definitely the cause of their strife. Annalise looked at him.

"Do you think the MacDonald could have killed Cassandra?"

"I do, why?"

"What if it were Snow. You said it yourself that she is obsessed and jealous. She could do anything to try and get you back, even murder."

"I can see it, but you don't understand the wrath of the Macleod's. My clan won't easily accept that it wasn't a MacDonald. They are still unaware as to why there was a sudden change with the wedding. They knew Snow, and now they know you and accept you."

"She was a lady here, which is why I am bringing it up to you. Cassandra didn't like her and they held no love with each other, so why wouldn't she be behind this? Lachlan, she was willing to attack me in the corridor and she made my first few days in the castle hell. She is twisted Lachlan, please look into this and investigate it."

CHAPTER TWENTY-FIVE

A MOMENT OF PEACE SETTLED OVER THE CLAN, THE AFTER Christmas grog was being passed around and some of the families continued the celebration until the next day even. Some activities were beginning to happen in preparation for Spring. First, Lachlan and his brothers disappeared with his father Llyr for a time, and when Annalise questioned them Lachlan simply said that it was better she didn't know what was being said in the meeting. Annalise could only guess that it was something about Snow and the circumstances behind Cassandra's death. There was one person among the brothers that could and would be willing to give her information, he'd gone as far as warn her about the fae and Tuatha dé Danann. About the spell that had been cast on Lachlan when he couldn't remember.

She caught Ethan outside with a woman, and the man nearly knocked her over when he noticed Annalise.

"What the hell woman!" Ethan said and the young woman squeaked, curtsied to Annalise, and left.

Annalise couldn't help but smirk, her cheeks warm. "I am

sorry Ethan. I didn't know this was your usual tupping grounds."

Ethan straightened his kilt and started to walk. Annalise followed.

"I was hoping to talk with you about something."

"If it's about anything that has to do with our meetings, I am not to tell you anything," Ethan told her.

Annalise felt her hopes dash at that, but it sounded like there was a hidden meaning in that sentence.

"However, I wouldn't be surprised if you found a certain hidden room where you could listen in," Ethan said as they walked.

Annalise thought for a moment and then said, "Where would one look if they were to hypothetically find this room?"

"One would go into the meeting room, and behind the tapestry is a hidden room, a closet really and there one would listen in," Ethan told her. "I must go, meeting again at noon."

He walked off, stopped and turned to her. "Don't get caught."

Annalise nodded and went on her own way. It was nearly noon and she wanted to be there before they started just as Ethan had told her. She would find out what they were hiding and then if it were important and needed to be discussed she would make sure they told her everything, she was just as much an important person in this situation. She'd been attacked by Snow, and she had watched Cassandra die. Why not include her? If it was because she was a woman she was going to be pissed.

Annalise walked into the room and found the tapestry where just as Ethan said was the closet. She opened it, and quickly climbed inside. It was roomy and smelled of roses and sandalwood. Her instincts told her to run, but she stayed where she was, information was more important than her fear and wanting to run. She heard the sound of footsteps and chairs being moved, and finally male voices. She recognized Lachlan's at once, and Kieran, Ethan, and Llyr's followed.

She strained to hear as they began a discussion about the MacDonald, and that topic was the only one that Annalise could sit through. Nothing about Snow and sure as hell nothing about anything more. Just talk of the MacDonald so far. Annalise's eyelids fell for a few seconds and she fell asleep. In the dream she was trying to catch Lachlan, but every time she got closex, he would fly away with those magnificent black and white wings.

"I will have to send her back," she heard Lachlan said and Annalise jerked awake. She moved to the door and put her ear to it trying to chase the sleep from her mind. "Things will get worse, we know this. If anything happened to Annalise, I couldn't live with myself."

"Yes, but Snow could follow her to the modern time, and she would not be protected," she heard Llyr say. "I certainly wouldn't protect a human, but Annalise is an exception. She is different. I like her."

"Good to know, Father. However, I would take the chance of the authorities there in that time. I will keep Snow here, and if she killed Cassandra, we will bring her to justice. Let her come back to us. As for the MacDonald, it seems to be too quiet over there. I don't like it," Lachlan explained.

"Neither do I," Kieran said, his voice filled with disgust. "They are planning something Lachlan, if we just have a spy within the clan we could know."

"I already discussed this with you, I am not going to send anyone to the MacDonald's to spy on them. We will be the neutral clan, if they are planning something and if it comes to our doorstep, we will then take care of it. For now, we can only speculate and without the proof I need, both Snow and the MacDonald's are innocent and those outside of our castle would see that too and not take a chance and let us mete out justice," Lachlan said.

He was trying to convince the others not to jump the gun for it seems Kieran was looking for a fight, but that seemed appropriate for he had been struck with a rock. Someone had thrown it, and that someone was one John MacDonald. Annalise sighed, this feud they had was ridiculous.

Danu walked her realm and basked in the sun, the smell of roses and peonies in the air. She loved spring, and having the eternal spring was nice, and comforting. She'd hated being in the cold underground when her people had been driven under the earth with their fae counterparts. They were fae in a sense, but they called themselves the Tuatha dé Danann, and they were higher than most fae. The gods and goddesses, and it was Danu's job to govern her fae children and human worshippers. She'd been going after Annalise for a long time and had wanted to work with her. So, she'd sent the woman signs, a lot of signs. Starting from the time of her birth to womanhood Annalise noticed the signs but hadn't connected them to Danu. She was a mostly forgotten goddess to those who weren't in the pagan community. Not since everything about religion changed. Once she was worshipped, loved and given gifts by everyone. Now, it was a select few. This did not anger or sadden Danu. It was the way of life, everything had a cycle, even gods and goddesses.

Danu looked into the water in her scrying bowl, she watched as a woman with long black hair and pale skin made plans with a clan known to have a feud with the Macleods.

What she was doing there, the goddess had no idea, only that her instincts told her that she should be protecting Annalise.

"Edith," Danu called

The little fate, Edith, came into her room and curtsied. "My lady."

"I would like for you to watch this woman. Something isn't sitting with her, and I would like to know what we are dealing with."

Edith looked at the woman in the scrying bowl and made a mental note of her features. She nodded, closed her eyes and transported herself to the woman. She watched her from afar, invisible to the woman. The worst that could happen is that the woman would feel a slight breeze where Edith had been.

"Lachlan won't see it coming, the MacDonalds are nearly ready for their first raid of this battle dear Joseph, and soon those Tuatha dé Danann will be in the ground once more and Otherworld will be mine, then Lachlan will want to be with me."

"I want to be with you my lady," Joseph told her. "If you would give me the chance."

"Silence! There is someone here," Snow said and Edith froze.

Snow walked over to where Edith stood, and stooped down to her level. "I can smell you, little fate, but cannot see you. Why don't you show yourself and join us. Working for those Tuatha dé Danann must be exhausting."

Edith almost didn't see the sword coming as Joseph attacked her, the spell breaking just as Edith moved away trying to escape. She closed her eyes and willed herself back to Danu's side.

"What happened?" Danu asked.

"She knows about me, about you lady. She is after the Tuatha dé Danann and plans to take over the Otherworld.

Annalise is not safe. You must tell someone my lady." Edith felt her heart race. She'd nearly been killed, not that a fate could die as long as they stayed a fate, but it still hurt very much.

"I will send Manna to Lachlan. We will figure this out, even if that means I have to get more involved," Danu told the small fate. "I am sorry I put you in so much danger Edith."

"I will continue to gather information about her, Lady. You focus on Annalise. I don't want Manna to be reborn in a world with that woman in charge," Edith explained.

Danu nodded, and sent for Manna. The oldest fate came in a blink of an eye and stared at her youngest sister. Manna didn't have to know what happened for she was well versed in the Otherworld and its happenings, having perfected scrying long before any of her sisters. She'd watched Snow and Edith and found that she didn't like it. This really messed with her possibility of being born.

"I will go now. I feel that talking with Lachlan is important at this time. However, Annalise will need to stay ignorant and in the dark for the moment," Manna said. "I have seen this."

Danu nodded. "Do what you must."

CHAPTER TWENTY-SIX

Manna found Lachlan in his meeting room overlooking the gardens below. It was like a ping of magic shot through her as she crossed into the room and the wards that Lachlan had cast upon the room to help him detect presences other than human.

"What do you want, spirit?" he asked.

Manna froze and didn't know what to say. She was a girl of tall stature, and with long purple hair pulled back into a bow. Different from the little girl Lachlan kept seeing every day since Annalise had come into his life. She seemed like she was getting older, and that unsettled Lachlan more than a little because he feared she was aging too fast.

"If you've come to stop the life cycle, I cannot help you. You will need to grow old and go to Awen on your own, I am afraid, and become reborn," Lachlan explained.

"I will be reborn my laird, to you and Lady Annalise. I hope to be a great daughter," Manna told him.

Lachlan just stared at her and then finally said, "I have seen you so long fate, why now have you come to me and spoken to me?"

Manna gave him a grimace. "I was scared to come forward. I was not ready to be reborn and I tried everything to not have to be. Showing myself to you was the only way I could come to realize that my fate has always been rebirth. This is not why I come to you, this is about a woman named Snow. She hopes to destroy your clan and the Tuatha dé Danann. You know the mother goddess has watched over you and your own, but she hasn't the power to defeat Snow."

Lachlan snorted. "She's a goddess. She is more powerful than Snow. Besides, I am not concerned about that woman and if she does try and attack us, we will be ready for them."

"Macleod, this is not the time to become stubborn. You must watch your backs or else I will not be reborn," Manna told him.

Lachlan wanted to feel bad for the young girl, and his mind screamed that she was right, but his clan were looking toward the horizon for the MacDonalds not Snow. They thought she was a woman who spurned their laird and nothing more.

"If you are reborn, you will do so with me and Annalise, you are certain?"

Manna rolled her eyes and shook her head in that way that teenagers did when someone asked them a stupid question. "Honestly, among humans I have a hard time understanding why they don't listen, and now I am inclined to believe that the Tuatha dé Danann children cannot listen. Llyr meddled with your memory, and Snow sent you back to a time you wanted to forget. I think it's time that you changed that for the better. It will not happen again. You get one chance Lachlan Macleod, one chance or you will lose all you love." Manna shook her head again. "And don't go spouting this to Annalise either. If she knew about me, she would definitely try to stay beside you."

With that said Manna was gone, and Lachlan was left to

think about what the fate had just said to him. Being Tuatha dé Danann was hard at times and choices had to be made. Such as the one he had to make, Annalise must be sent back to the modern time and not allowed to return. He walked over to his library and pulled down a box. Inside it was a lone black and white feather that he found where Annalise sat naked outside Dunvegan castle after she'd been hurled through time. For a Tuatha dé Danann, that journey was annoying at best, but to a human it must have felt like hell, and Lachlan was willing to put Annalise through hell just to make sure that she was back at home. Did he want the fate as his daughter? Yes, but only if that meant that Annalise was no longer here in 1490, he didn't want her to see the bloodshed that could be spilled once Snow was caught and the killer of Cassandra was executed.

Lachlan stared at the feather and hoped that it would disintegrate by the time Annalise knew he'd used it on her and went back for it. He would have it encased in amber so that when the time came, he could slip it around her neck and then she would be gone from this part of the world and back in her own.

Danu looked at Manna as the young woman returned. It was so hard to see that conversation between Lachlan and her. Had she known that Manna was afraid? She hadn't been aware that fates could have emotions and attitudes. They were mostly expressionless and bland, but this was the first time she got to see a fate as they transitioned into being reborn. It was a rare sight to behold, and sad as well. The story goes that when a fate found their mothers they would transition from a child into an adult and eventually into an old woman and disappear. No one knew just exactly what they went through after that transition. Was it instantaneous?

Danu wished she could feel what it felt to be reborn, but as a goddess she was meant to rule over her people, and to answer a prayer here and there, and make sure the fates three were being taken care of. Since not many people knew her, she was regulated to babysitting. All the gods and goddesses had their human or creature to look after but only the ones who were not well known were to take care of the fates three and their areas of expertise. A fate was an honor, but annoying as the girls or boys turned into children from a baby and learned to talk. Those days are what Danu lived for, learning all she could about the world through their eyes, and live it through them. She was the mother, and as fae, Danu could live the lives they lived but not see the process of the transition.

CHAPTER TWENTY-SEVEN

Lachlan watched Annalise pacing their room for the hundredth time...Hell, he'd lost count a long time ago. Lachlan chuckled, and Annalise whirled around to look at him. "What's so funny?" she asked.

"Nothing, it's just you look so beautiful when you are thinking. I love it," Lachlan said.

Annalise smiled, "Thanks, but what about the wedding, so much is being planned and I am so busy I feel like I could pass out. I mean honestly Lachlan, can't we cut this down to a small wedding, friends and family and no more?"

"I know you are worried, but inviting our allies will show them that the Macleods are folk that are friendly, and our wedding is what will make the clan chiefs happy. To see their fellow laird marry, is a great honor. Also, the bond needs realignment to determine the line that will connect our souls."

"That's what I fear most, what happens if you go to war someday and I see you die or feel you die? What then?"

"I can see what you mean, but I don't think it works that way. Why, did you feel anything within our bond?"

Annalise shook her head "No, but what if I do, you said yourself that no one truly knows about the bond only that it guides them to their true mate and can be severed if you were a fate."

"Love come and lay in bed with me, stop worrying about all this all will be well." Lachlan adjusted so his hairy leg showed, and he bit his lip, tried to make flirty face but instead was looking like a flamingo in a bed.

Annalise burst out laughing. "What are you trying to do?"

"Be sexy. You do this when we are about to make love. I thought to, maybe, do so myself."

"Lachlan, you aren't sexy, looking like that."

"Like what?"

"Like a bear having a hard time farting."

Lachlan roared with laughter and turned in the bed as he couldn't help himself. Annalise followed and was almost blindsided when Lachlan flashed before her in his naked splendor his black and white wings flashing behind him. Annalise walked over to him and touched the feathers.

"So soft, like cotton," she said.

"Tuatha dé Danann have wings, but only some of us actually use them and some are not allowed to use them without a special permit."

"Can you tell me more about your people?" Annalise asked.

"After I make love to you. I've always wanted to cover your naked body with my wings while I make love to you," Lachlan said.

Annalise screamed out when Lachlan grabbed her and pulled her into a deep kiss. Annalise moaned as he pulled her around and lay her on her back. Lachlan covered her with his wings at that moment, and Annalise smiled as the feathers caressed her skin. Lachlan smiled at her, and pulled his long hair into a tie, and kissed her thoroughly. He had her moaning by the time he began the real play, and Annalise shattered as she felt a completeness, so complete that she knew all would be well.

Edith, and Ailish watched as their sister Manna become a woman with breasts! Manna covered her breasts with her tattered shirt and realized that the transition had finally started. Soon she would be gone from her sisters and a new fate would be born a month after her birth. He or she would be her mate should the bond be broken between another fated mate as the fates themselves had rules and could choose to reject a mate. This practice was kept only to the fates as they believed humans, and other paranormal beings would want to reject a mate of the bond no matter what.

"Sister, you cannot leave us," Edith said.

"Good riddance, at least one of us gets to go on to the transitioning," Ailish said.

Manna smiled at her sisters and gave them each a hug. "I know this is hard, but we knew it would happen and grateful we all must be. Take care of yourselves and of the new lad or lass and we will see each other again, someday."

Annalise hated when he lured her with sex and changed her mind. It was dirty, and a bit underhanded. She looked at the now sleeping Lachlan and tried her best not to have to get out of bed into the cold air to pee. She hated cold nights because it was harder to find the restroom when she had to pee and not freeze to death. Finally, Annalise got up and made her way out of the room in search for the bathroom. As she was getting near to it, she was stopped by a beautiful young woman with purple hair, she giggled and led Annalise the rest of the way to the restroom. Dunvegan was haunted, she'd known from the moment she'd entered the castle in her time. She had just now saw the ghost of Dunvegan or a ghost of Dunvegan castle. Annalise got many different gifts on the way back to Lachlan, the same young woman laughing and guiding her down to their room.

Annalise stopped and looked at the woman. "Listen, if you've nothing better to do then I suggest you find someone else to haunt."

"Who says I am a ghost, Mother?" the woman said.

Annalise raised an eyebrow and stared at the woman. "What do you mean, Mother?"

"You're my mother or will be. I just had to come and get another glance at you and judge for myself."

"And your judgement?" Annalise asked.

"I find you will make a great mother, and I am looking forward to being born. Here, have this," said the woman, throwing Annalise a box and vanishing.

Annalise opened the box and found a piece of the tux that Joseph Declan had worn in 2019. How could that be? Joseph couldn't be here. The man who attacked her before certainly looked like Joseph, but her mind couldn't grasp that Joseph was here and that he too had changed. But this tux piece meant something. Why would her future daughter, if that is what she was and not some demon, come to play tricks on her. This place truly was an enigma, and it was frustrating.

CHAPTER TWENTY-EIGHT

Lachlan found Llyr waiting near the fairy bridge. He stood there tall and proud, and naked, his webbed wings out in the cool night air. Lachlan tried not to be ashamed of seeing his father this way, but the Tuatha dé Danann did what they wanted and Lachlan was not going to go against his father, he was part human after all.

"There has been a clue," Lachlan told him

Llyr half-turned and put out his hand palm up. Lachlan put the piece of cloth into his hand, and Llyr turned back around toward the full moon, and inspected the piece of cloth. It had the faint smell of perfume, and no other clues on it

"What makes you think this is a clue?" Llyr asked his son. "Have I not taught you better than this?"

"You taught me not to overlook the small things. Don't you have spell you can use that can find the person that this belongs too?" Lachlan asked.

"It doesn't work like that, and I am not a dog, magic can detect a genetic signature, but it cannot be used to go after a person without cause. The Tuatha dé Danann will not allow it."

Lachlan nodded, and didn't press the issue. The elder Tuatha dé Danann were grumpy at best and they could do things on a whim. Llyr was Tuatha dé Danann and one of the oldest. He had a wealth of knowledge and he could call upon centuries of information. That, coupled with his magic, were a powerful force. Llyr had his own realm, but was the only god who didn't encourage worshippers. He was modest and dangerous, all at once.

"You know what's best, Father."

Llyr didn't say a word, spread his wings, and flew off into the light of the moon. He would go to that realm now, a realm that Lachlan couldn't venture to until the day he died. He wasn't sure he even wanted to be a part of that realm when he passed on. From old texts, Llyr's realm was in darkness, and so those who worshipped him, worshipped the darkness. He wasn't even sure if those texts were reliable as they had been written by confused men drunk on alcohol, likely whiskey.

Llyr's battle had been having to give up their children, and he did as she said would happen and sent them off to another realm, one where his people were known as myths and legends. Stories people had come with to keep their kids in line. Pathetic really, no one in that realm even knew there was another world just connected to theirs through doors that were looked after by 8 guardians. They were chosen, and because Llyr had been tasked to give his first-born son as one of the guardians, and because of that, Llyr had to send his children far from the Otherworld. Llyr found a spot to land, one with almost no people to see him. He walked over to a shimmery and sparkly part of the forest that he walked into, beyond was a door with intricate knot design. This was the doorway to the modern realm, here Llyr could be anyone he wanted. Beyond that door was freedom that only a few from the Otherworld has tasted. Llyr walked through the door's many spells, undetected. Lachlan wouldn't know about the intrusion. His guardian senses couldn't sense someone as powerful as Llyr.

The pull into the modern world thrilled him as he traveled through a tunnel of colors and memories. They sparkled across the tunnel, even those of the present, he saw his son's memories and again felt that pang of regret, but it was brief and surrounded in a heart of stone in a matter of seconds. Llyr adjusted the suit he conjured around him, and walked through the night like a phantom. No one here but those with the sight could see him or interact with him. He had just the person he was seeing that night and found a man who called himself James. A pict, and fae who had a library's work full of technology and books. He owned his own tactical company, and dozens of other businesses in the realm. He also knew that Llyr had taken Lachlan back to the Otherworld.

"Where is my daughter Llyr, I know you have her or know if she is in Otherworld," James demanded as his men let Llyr into the meeting room.

"All in good time," Llyr told James.

"Annalise isn't some pawn you can use in your stupid games."

"She isn't a pawn, she is a guest of honor. Besides, I think perhaps she could be home anytime if you can help me identify where this came from," Llyr explained and gave James the cloth.

James growled and snatched the cloth from his hand. "I will have my daughter back and then I am coming for you."

Llyr returned back to Dunvegan castle and gave Lachlan the news, to say his son was thrilled was an understatement, he was actually very mad. James hadn't been the wealth of information that Llyr had hoped to get. It seemed like even the best books, technology and magic could only get so much these days. Llyr walked into his room later that night and found Danu standing before his bed, naked but only a see-through silk robe on.

Lachlan looked over the finished product, and then looked at Llyr. "You're sure that this will send Annalise back to her time?"

Llyr snorted. "If you don't believe me then do it now and send her home."

Lachlan shook his head, and pocketed the feather now encased in amber. He thanked Llyr and went to his room where he put the feather in a sporran he didn't use in his wardrobe. Lachlan needed to wait until the time was right, but if he didn't send her home soon then he wouldn't ever send her home. His resolve was not very good when it came to Annalise, she made his knees weak and his stomach all fluttery and, damn it, he loved it. Lachlan wanted nothing more than to bury himself inside Annalise and never leave. He felt bad that he had to send her back, but he knew he had to.

Lachlan's room door opened and he expected Annalise but instead his brother Ethan stood in the door.

"What happened?" Lachlan asked.

"We got word that the MacDonald is on the move," he said.

Lachlan nodded and dismissed him and went to find Annalise. He found her in the garden at Cassandra's grave talking to it as if the woman was still alive. He walked over to her and put his hand on her shoulder as he looked at the grave.

"She is in a better place," he told Annalise.

She nodded and stood and turned to look at Lachlan. "I miss her."

Lachlan nodded and led her back into the castle and escorted her to our room. I told her to close her eyes for a surprise.

"Lachlan what is this about?"

"Shh....Just lay back and enjoy," he told her.

She did as she was told. Lachlan undressed and then moved onto the bed. He crawled over to her and slowly began to undress her as well, kissing her on her neck, and downward as he freed her breasts. They popped out of her bodice, and he pulled one into his mouth and sucked on it. Annalise moaned, and his cock hardened. He pulled the dress from her lifting her up and falling.

"Well I thought this would be a great idea," he told Annalise.

Annalise laughed and lifted her butt to allow him to pull the rest of her dress off her body. He marveled over her body, her porcelain skin shown bright and flushed from his loving.

"Open your eyes lass," he told her.

Annalise opened her eyes and he moved between her legs and thrust into her. Annalise arched her back in a scream, and he hesitated but then she looked at him with that look in her eyes and he pulled out and thrust again, this time harder. Annalise moaned and her nails bit his back. His little vixen loved to be fucked hard. He set a hard pace and soon they were sweating, thier bodies soaked. He poured into her, and Annalise rode his orgasm with her own. He lay his head on her chest, still inside her and gave lazy kisses on her breasts.

"One for the son and another for the daughter," he said.

"How many children you want Lachlan?"

He looked at Annalise, the topic of children never came up before. "I want at least two, a boy and a girl."

"I want the same," she said.

Lachlan smiled. "You shall have it, and I will enjoy giving them to you, my love."

Annalise sighed, and Lachlan closed his eyes. All was right in his world right now, and he wouldn't have it any other way. *I would kill for this woman, I would die for her*, he thought.

CHAPTER TWENTY-NINE

Danu walked over to Llyr ever so slowly, and when she got to him, she pushed back a stray hair from his face. "Still handsome as before, but alas still the fool you've always been."

Llyr growled, "What do you want goddess?"

"For you to stop your search and allow things to fall into place," Danu told him.

Llyr snarled, "So you are a part of this, I should have known another Tuatha dé Danann was involved."

"I have been involved since the day Lachlan, your son, was born," Danu told him. "In fact, I was among the women who gave birth to many of your children."

Nothing was secret when it came to the damn Tuatha dé Danann deities. They either knew what was happening or turned a blind eye toward the fact. Llyr hated them for it, he'd had to send his children to another realm just so they could live a normal life away from those in the deity families couldn't mock or use them.

"Is that all you wish for me? To back off and allow your little game to play out?" Llyr asked.

Danu smiled. "I would be eternally grateful, and it makes my job just a little easier."

Llyr crossed his arms and nodded. Danu laughed, and gave a small clap. "Thanks so much Llyr, you won't be disappointed."

Llyr shook his head. "Thanks for your presence, mother goddess."

"I am a bit disappointed that the cloth yielded no information. Strange that the magic wouldn't detect anything," Lachlan told Llyr while they met in the drawing room of Dunvegan castle.

"Perhaps my magic isn't as strong as it used to be," Llyr lied.

Lachlan nodded, he wasn't well versed in magic. He knew just enough that he could get by and do his duties as a guardian. Most of all, he wouldn't argue with Llyr.

"I do not know what we are going to do about the killer, so far the MacDonalds haven't come forward, and neither has Snow or Joseph, her little lackey," Lachlan said. "If I had some idea maybe I could get a head start."

Llyr winced and felt the pang again and thought maybe he shouldn't be lying to his own son, but Danu having appeared to him meant that his plans were on a thin line and that the goddess knew what he was doing. As a high deity, Danu could scry anytime she wanted. She saw all because she was the mother goddess and therefore all of her children had to be watched everyday. The fates three helped her with her duties as each god or goddess of the Awen had a fates three. Children bred and born to be fates, ultimate children who could choose to end or begin a life.

"I must get back to Annalise, she is going mad with all of

the planning for the wedding," Lachlan said and excused himself. Llyr gave him a quick bow as he left.

Llyr himself turned and looked at the piece of silk that hung on the wall. The Fairy flag, with the wave of this flag the fae would come, and the Macleod would win any battle three times. It had been used already so it meant that the flag had two waves left until the magic faded. Ironic that his sister had struck that bargain with the Macleod Laird in the past. Their children had gone on to have their own families and each of them had a great fae power. One of the powerful fae families, boasting highest honor from their gods and goddesses or not at all. If Danu was correct, Lachlan would need to do something drastic to stop what was coming.

Lachlan found Annalise in their quarters wearing naught but her chemise as she picked out decorations. Ribbon, clothing, and other odds and ends filled the room and their bed. Annalise turned and looked at him.

"Thank the gods," Annalise said.

Lachlan smiled and found something to do. Later that night, Annalise showed him just how grateful she was. The next morning, Lachlan found himself amid a bed of ribbon, and jumped when he noticed it wasn't a bed of ribbon but of his hair full of the stuff. He looked at Annalise and nearly laughed. She lay back on the bed naked, her hair covered in ribbon and coal drawn on her face in funny smiling faces and animals. Just what had they done last night?

"I think we made a mess of the decorations," Annalise whispered and Lachlan laughed and gave her a deep kiss.

"We need to get up," Lachlan told her.

Annalise stretched, and shook her head. "A few more minutes."

"We can't sleep all day love, we've wedding to plan for, and I want to ensure that you have my help should you ever need it," Lachlan told her.

CHAPTER THIRTY

"THE MACDONALD ARE TO BLAME, THIS IS THE ONLY ANSWER my son." Llyr said that morning,

Annalise, who insisted she sit in on the conversation, shook her head. "Snow is the enemy here, she attacked us once before and you know that she would again. She is not sane."

Lachlan dismissed her. He was tired of her mentioning Snow every time he saw her. The woman had begun an obsession that was getting very rampant.

"There must be proof of your claims. I cannot be rash here my love. I need proof," Lachlan told her again. "Telling me this over and over again is just causing a lot of annoyance."

"Well maybe you should stop the feud with the MacDonalds!" Annalise said crossing her arms.

Llyr looked at her as if she were crazy.

"I would like to think this over, until then this matter is squashed. No more talking of it," Lachlan said. "We will get our answers soon. When I know something, you will too."

Annalise sat back and brooded, and Llyr just shook his

head. At least he'd managed to thwart any more talk of Snow and the MacDonalds. Annalise would still be a problem.

Lachlan decided to go out on his own that night. He told Llyr and Annalise he needed a ride so he could clear his head. Annalise had not been happy and pestered him about going and talking about 'the wedding'.

Lachlan rode for an hour and was hit with the stench of death. Another moment and he found the body of a young woman about seventeen, from her plaid he could discern that she was from the MacDonald clan. Lachlan winced as he looked over her body and found the slit on her neck. She had been beaten too, and her face was unrecognizable. He wouldn't be able to send her likeness home to her family so they could identify her. She had been dead for a day, and this proved to him that even the MacDonalds were having a hard time of it all. They had a killer in their midst, just as the Macleod did.

This meant that the MacDonalds were at least having problems, and because of that, it was likely that they had nothing to do with Cassandra's death. Snow seemed the logical choice in all of this, she did attack them in the other time period, but did that still mean that Elaine would attack them here? She had been the love of his life at one time before she died. Problem with Elaine was that she didn't stay dead, claiming to be reborn as Snow. This was all so complicated.

Lachlan called Llyr into the drawing room later on that night, and told him what he found, and the Tuatha dé Danann prince didn't seem happy.

"We cannot continue the feud knowing that the MacDonald's are dealing with the same killer," Lachlan said.

"Stopping the feud will change nothing, there would still be a killer."

"But at least they will have the help of the Macleod."

"You have got to stop killing Joseph, you keep calling attention to yourself," Snow admonished.

Joseph looked at her. "You made me this way."

Snow put a hand on his cheek. "I know my sweet, but now is not the time to going on a killing rampage, reign it in or it will your blood covering that shirt."

Joseph backed off and closed his eyes. He wanted to stop the killing, but it was like an impulse he couldn't resist. Everyone he had killed so far had deserved it. A MacDonald lass who was going to alert the laird of her clan, she had looked so much like Annalise. When had his life become so full of madness? Before Snow, he'd had it all, a company and a woman he thought had been the one. But life seemed to screw him again, and instead of Annalise, he got Snow. He smelled, tasted and breathed Snow. She was his so called 'mate'. Just because he felt a certain way about Snow didn't mean it would change him, not at all. He was Joseph Declan, billionaire and mogul. He still wanted Annalise O'Callaghan.

"Don't worry love, we will be free soon," Snow said laying her head onto his chest.

Snow wanted to also feel happy that Joseph had accepted her being his mate but she found that he wasn't Lachlan, and she missed being in his embrace. The warmth she felt emanating off of him, and no matter what fate said Lachlan Macleod would forever be her mate, fuck Joseph Declan! Peace fell onto the room and soon Snow was asleep and dreaming of her wedding to Lachlan.

Later, Joseph watched through the mirror at Annalise, a memory of her when they'd been together. She was so happy in this image, and Joseph winced. He had been the reason for their breakup. He had abused her and for that she had left him. He just wanted the chance to tell her how incredibly sorry he was. But she wasn't listening, words and gifts weren't enough now, and he needed action.

Joseph looked the woman trembling before him. She had tasted sweet when he had slept with her, all consensual until she realized just what he was. A monster, and this monster wanted blood. She whimpered and Joseph felt the excitement coursing through him. He slit her throat with his dagger.

"How long have they been missing?" Annalise asked.

Lachlan grimaced. "Almost three weeks."

Annalise shook her head, that poor woman and her child. Those people who were turning up dead. "Do you think they are alright?"

Lachlan shrugged. "Given the recent killing of a young MacDonald lass, I really cannot say."

Annalise nodded and took it as that. No one knew what they would do about this, or rather what they could do about this. There was no trace of the child or lady of the MacDonald clan. It was like they disappeared as if by magic. Magic, the Otherworld was different from the modern time, here they used magic daily as if it were a hot commodity, and despite the occasional finger pointing and the calls that a witch had been found, it was a peaceful world.

"Soon love, we will be back to normal and your book will be published, and we can get away from Otherworld and back to the modern time. I think it would do you good," Lachlan said.

"Ugh Lachlan, you just had to remind me of the book. I have hit a snag and damn."

"What sort of snag?"

"Something about the story, I cannot decide just what the love interest is."

"I assume it would be a man," Lachlan said.

"It is a man, but I cannot decide if he should be a magical being or just a human."

"I think the exciting thing should be the relationship between the two."

Annalise looked at him and smiled. "You know just what to say to bring me back around to the positives. I love you Lachlan."

"I love you lass, now get your ass over here so I can ravish you with my love."

CHAPTER THIRTY-ONE

LATE THAT NIGHT AFTER A LONG LOVEMAKING SESSION WITH Lachlan, Annalise got up hoping that the kitchen had something to eat. She was starved and didn't know why. She found an apple, and a small loaf of leftover bread. Annalise ate as she walked around and came to the door that would lead Annalise to the garden. She had been spending more time there since Cassandra died. She looked out the window and narrowed her gaze on the woman standing in the garden at Cassandra's grave. Annalise recognized the black as night hair, and pale skin. Snow. She dropped her bread and ran out into the garden. Annalise slapped her face when she got to her and she flinched only for a moment before smiling at her, her red as blood lips shining in the moonlight.

"Oh Annalise, what a show and a skilled hand. I felt pain for the first time," Snow said to her.

"What are you doing here?" Annalise said when she really should have called for the guards and had her arrested. But she felt strong at the moment, and she didn't want to back down. Annalise had enough.

Snow looked over Annalise's shoulder, and she turned to

find Joseph standing behind her with rope, and a bag. She knew then that she was in trouble. She drew the small dagger that she carried with her at all times, after Cassandra had died she had taken Lachlan up on some training. Snow laughed at Annalise and her mini dagger. It wasn't a lot, but it was deadly and she knew just what spot she could hit that would kill her instantly. Annalise moved to swing her arm, but Snow blew some pink powder in her face. Annalise's world went dark and crashed.

When Annalise woke up again, she was watching Snow in front of a mirror with people walking around. What time was it? How long has she been here? Annalise looked around and took stock of her surroundings. She was in a room, with a four-post bed big enough to fit eight, the mirror, an enormous fireplace with a fire, and a table where Joseph sat watching her. She shifted to get the pressure off her arms as she was lying on her back. Joseph stood and walked over to Annalise and helped her up.

"You'll feel a little groggy, the spell takes a lot out of you," Joseph told Annalise.

Annalise nodded, and she fell back to sleep. When she woke again, Snow was with Joseph on the bed having sex. Annalise closed her eyes again, and when she woke up again, it jolted her awake, the sound of screams. Annalise stared at the mirror and watched in horror as a battle unfolded before her eyes.

"The battle of Glendale, your man will waive the fairy flag any moment now and when that happens, I will give you this, and we will be sent home, you without your memories, and me with a wife," Joseph told Annalise as he walked over to her from the table. He showed Annalise a vial that was green and dazzling. "I worked very hard for this potion, and I won't waste it."

Annalise squirmed and tried to push away from Joseph,

but he laughed and watched the mirror again. She watched as the battle went on, and finally Lachlan stood in the drawing room and there, on the wall, he took down a tattered piece of fabric, and with a wave he invoked its magic and Annalise closed her eyes as the tears streamed down her face. Annalise felt Joseph behind her, and grabbing her mouth and forcing her to open my mouth and pouring the liquid down her throat. Annalise sputtered and coughed. She didn't care anymore, Lachlan had waved the fairy flag, he was likely gone looking for her now. The battle was won, and now was the time to go searching. He wouldn't find her. Annalise didn't know where she was, and Lachlan would likely have a hard time finding her as well because Joseph had made Annalise drink the potion.

Annalise felt a little fuzzy, and then she jerked forward and hurled through a tunnel like the one she had been in when she had come to Dunvegan. Annalise landed in the snow, crying out as she cracked her head on a rock. Annalise lay there and closed her eyes and waited for Joseph to come and get her, but there was nothing. Annalise opened her eyes and looked around. She was in a forest, and the snow was deep. Annalise struggled with her bonds, and tried to slip her hands free, but Joseph had done a good job. He always did. That was what he had liked. Annalise heard the footsteps before she saw her, a beautiful woman with long white hair and almost tan skin.

CHAPTER THIRTY-TWO

THE BATTLE WAS HEATED AND RAW, LACHLAN KNEW THAT WITH the forces, Donald MacDonald had that the Macleod clan were outnumbered. More and more of his people died at the hands of the MacDonald who lay waste to their land and came to Dunvegan Castle. Not only did they threaten the land, but also his woman, Annalise. They'd kidnapped her and wanted to exchange her for the daughter of the laird of MacDonald but the Macleods didn't have her. So, in response to their demands to get Annalise back the MacDonald's laid waste to their land. Dunvegan and the Macleod's would prevail; Lachlan would make sure of that. He called upon his Tuatha dé Danann magic and sent it out to his clansmen. He hoped the added strength would help them through this battle.

Annalise struggled with her bonds and finally managed to free herself. She watched the MacDonald as he walked around the camp not paying attention to her. She felt her fae magic rise in her body, and Annalise closed her eyes and hoped to become invisible. The man was alerted to her movements and ran over to her but started looking around and shouting. Annalise walked over to a water barrel and snickered. She really was invisible!? She loved this fae magic! Annalise crept away from them and ran toward the direction where she thought Lachlan was. She ran as fast as her legs could carry her and managed to climb a hill when she saw a group of men and among those men, she saw the Macleod clansman, Murdo. Annalise ran the rest of the way.

"Wait! Don't leave me!" She called out and Murdo stopped his horse.

Murdo turned to face her and his eyes widened, Annalise was relieved and collapsed onto the ground as Murdo kicked his horse into a gallop and over to her. He swooped her up onto the saddle of the horse.

Lachlan got the call that Murdo Macaskil had returned and with him the lady Annalise Macleod. Lachlan swung up into his horse's saddle and kicked it into a fast trot and met Murdo and his men outside of the camp. Lachlan scooped Annalise into his arms from Murdo and rode with her back into camp. Lachlan got off his horse once he was at his tent and carried her into it where he lay her down on his pallet. Annalise was exhausted and was already out for the count. He walked back out of the tent and thanked Murdo and went back to Annalise. The war waged on throughout the day and all seemed lost for the Macleods. Lachlan and Murdo tried to formulate a plan but upon hearing that the MacDonalds had joined their clansmen from Clannald, they were at a loss.

Lachlan then had to come to a decision; it would be a hard one, but one that he knew would ensure the clan's victory. The only problem? He would not be remembered in this time except if one of the clan were Tuatha dé Danann or fae. As long as he was with Annalise it didn't matter if he was laird or not. Lachlan sent Murdo out with word of what he was about to do and prepared for the end of the war.

Lachlan woke Annalise later that night when all was quiet.

"What's wrong?" Annalise asked as Lachlan took her into his arms and transported her to the fairy pools where he'd proposed for the second time.

"Lachlan, why are we here?"

Lachlan pressed his lips to hers and slipped the necklace he'd made of one of his feathers.

"I'm sorry lass, please forgive me," he told her. "Know that I love you."

Annalise screamed out when Lachlan let her go and she felt herself being pulled away from him. She landed in a forest of snow-covered trees. A beautiful woman with glowing skin and long red hair stood before her.

"Welcome Annalise of the Seelie court, I am Danu, mother goddess."

Annalise stood amazed at Danu, she'd heard about the mother goddess during her time with the fae and her grandfather. Seelie court worshipped Danu, and said she was a beauty and they weren't wrong!

"Where am I?" Annalise asked.

Danu smiled. "Within my place, in Awen."

Annalise's eyes went wide. "I'm dead!?"

Danu laughed. "Goodness no, I just wanted to talk to you."

Annalise sighed in relief; good to know she wasn't dead. "What do we have to discuss Danu, I mean, mother goddess."

"Danu is fine, and it's about your mother."

"My mother?" Annalise asked.

"Yes, I want you to go back to when you were a child and save her," Danu explained. "If you do this, I cannot guarantee that you will see Lachlan again as he is Tuatha dé Danann."

Annalise's heart dipped, the ask was risky, but it was a chance to save her mother, in exchange for her true love.

"Everything in life comes with a consequence," Danu told her.

Annalise noted, a consequence. She'd lose her mother or possibly lose Lachlan.

"Can't you find fix this? Not that I don't love my mother, but how can you make me choose between two people I love?"

Danu thought for a second; she forgotten how frail Annalise was with her heart. She had been raised by Seelie living too long in the mortal realm.

"I can tell you that if you search for Lachlan, you may find him," Danu told her. "Not guaranteeing you will see him."

Annalise gave a small smile. Danu was going to give her a chance. The mother goddess was willing to break rules to make sure she could find Lachlan again.

"Then I'll go and save my mother."

Danu smiled and motioned to a dark part of the woods.

"Stay true to the path and follow the girl to your mother."

Annalise walked to the woods, took one look back at Danu who was nowhere to be found.

"Here we go," she whispered and walked into the darkness.

A bright purple, glowing girl took her by the hand and guided her through the darkness. They walked for what seemed like seconds and came out in front of the apartment she shared with her mother. The girl, now an old woman, smiled and faded into dust. Annalise was sad to see her go; she'd been around for a long while and Annalise felt like the girl was part of her own family.

Annalise entered the apartment, and everything seems smaller. She looked at her hands and gasped when she saw that her hands were a child's hands. She patted her body and found a mirror. It was true, she was a child again! This was what Danu had also meant about the consequences of her decisions. She'd have to relive a whole childhood again with her mother.

Annalise found her mother soaking in a bath, and she greeted her when she came in and Annalise couldn't believe how much she missed her mother when she heard the voice of an angel. Annalise wanted to cry and she did cry for Denyse jumped out of the tub got into a robe and gathered her into her arms. Annalise slept soundly that night in Denyse's arms, her only worry before she lay down was if Lachlan was doing well and if he survived the clan battle.

The next morning Annalise ate a big plate of pancakes, eggs, and bacon. Her first real meal since being back from the time tunnel. She was starving and it was likely due to her child's body needing the nutrients. Annalise's mother sat across the table from her and smiled as she ate.

"Slow down dear, you will choke," she told Annalise and she did as she was told.

"I have school today, will you be alright?" Annalise asked her.

Badb smiled and nodded, and Annalise hoped that it was true and that the killer didn't come early while she was having to relive her childhood again. Annalise stood and grabbed her backpack and kissed her on the cheek as she always had and went on her way.

Annalise relived school again and remembered the hardship of being a child. Bullies, teachers who didn't believe her when she told them she had to go home early to be with her mother. Couldn't do much when you were a child, and Annalise wondered why Danu had made her a child. She was weak. If it were not for Annalise's Seelie magic, and if that didn't work, then she would likely be doomed. Annalise ran back home after school and burst through the front door.

"Mom, I'm home!" Annalise called out to her.

"I am in the laundry room, can you be a dear and bring me your clothing so I can wash it?" she answered.

Annalise couldn't remember the last time she had done laundry. At Dunvegan, as lady of the castle, Annalise was not made to do chores. That was the maid's job. Annalise threw her bag onto the floor and ran to her room and grabbed her basket and carried it to her. Mom looked happy and was dancing a bit with headphones in her ears and she wondered if the technology of this time had ever shocked her. She was a Tuatha dé Danann after all.

"Do you want to go out tonight, mom? It's not so cold and we can eat at our favorite restaurant." Mom looked at Annalise and gave her a wink, and she laughed.

The next few days proved too demanding. They were on vacation for Christmas and Annalise had one more day to find out who the killer was and she had no luck researching or thinking who would want her mother dead. Tomorrow was the day, and Annalise was not ready for it. She snuggled into her mother's arms and celebrated Christmas with her and Dad. The only Christmas Annalise remembered being peaceful before all the hell broke loose.

CHAPTER THIRTY-THREE

Annalise woke up that Christmas Day and knew in her gut that today would be the day. It had happened about this time the first time, and she had found mom in the bathroom dead. She hadn't been as knowledgeable as she was now. She was not a normal child in this body, and she forced herself to go into the bathroom. Annalise knew from the police report that the killer hid in the apartment after everyone was gone for the day, playing in the snow. Annalise opened the bathroom door and walked in and sat on the toilet and waited. It was the longest wait, and she thought that something had changed, and that mom wouldn't be killed today, but Annalise was wrong for the window of the bathroom opened and a woman climbed inside. Her dark black hair looked frazzled, and the pit in Annalise's stomach grew wider when she saw the pale skin and finally the face of the woman, Snow. Snow was mom's killer?

Annalise hopped off the toilet and stared at her as she stared at Annalise.

"You better go back through that window if you know what's good for you," Annalise warned her.

Snow sneered. "I didn't expect you to be here, thought I came to the time of your birth. No matter, you're here now and I can be rid of you and that Tuatha dé Danann bitch!"

Annalise braced herself as Snow shot forth green flames from her hands and used her magic to strike back. Their magic collided and became one, and it was a battle of wills as they fought. She had never felt such power before. Annalise was still a beginner with her magic, and she was strong. Snow laughed as she pushed Annalise back, her tiny frame was no match to Snow's strength and Annalise was pushed up against the wall. She cried out and pushed herself and released more magic as she continued to barrage Annalise with the green flames. Annalise wouldn't let her kill her mother, wouldn't let her change her family forever. Annalise pushed back and moved her from her spot. Annalise laughed, and took a step, pushing Snow back little by little until she was against the wall of the bathroom, underneath the window. Snow called off her flames and Annalise called off her magic and they stared each other down.

"You are strong but not strong enough," Snow told Annalise and lunged at her, her hands in claws with long nails.

Annalise moved away but too late as her nails got her on my arm and ripped her sleeve and cut into her arm drawing blood. Annalise wanted to cry out, but she gritted her teeth and ran out of the bathroom. She heard Snow follow, and Annalise ran to the front door and outside the building and into the yard. Snow stepped into the snow and looked startled for a moment before coming after her. Annalise ran until her legs gave out and hid underneath some playground equipment.

"Come out, Annalise, come out. Come and play," Snow called out to her.

Annalise lay under the equipment and tried to regroup.

She had to find a way to stun her and then make sure that she was gone this time. She was a danger as long as she stayed here, and Annalise was the reason she was now outside in the neighborhood. She heard equipment crashing and took a deep breath and climbed out of her hiding spot.

"Hey bitch!" Annalise called out

Snow looked at Annalise, her face was now twisted into an ugly many toothed maw, her body tall and elongated and her nails claws. This was her authentic form, she wasn't even human. She ran at Annalise. Snow brought up her hands and conjured a ball of fire and sent it chasing after Annalise. It collided with her chest and she stumbled back and then got back up and came after Snow. Annalise lifted her hands in the air and imagined raining down swords at Snow. They appeared as she did so and pierced Snow's skin. Bloody Snow seemed unfazed, and Annalise had to do something, she was almost to Annalise. She closed her eyes and imagined Snow disappearing just as her hands touched her. Annalise opened her eyes to see her hands glowing a bright red and Snow stopped before her a shocked look on her monstrous face.

"How did you, you can't..." Snow tried to say, but she dissolved to ashes. She screamed it engulfed her and this time she was gone for good.

Annalise watched as the dust disappeared into the air and felt at peace for once in her entire life. It was then Annalise also realized that she had quite the story to tell. Annalise sat down on the bench in the park and just let herself relax before getting up and going back home where Badb waited for her with Lunasa. Annalise ran the rest of the way to the house and jumped into the older woman's arms.

"I thought I would never see you again," Annalise said to her.

Lunasa moved aside her hair. "I am your grandmother, why wouldn't I be here? I have gifts."

Annalise looked up at her and remembered. She wondered why she had been so friendly in Otherworld, and now she knew why. Her grandmother! Annalise smiled at her.

"You did good lass, you did good," she told her and scooped Annalise up in her arms and carried her into the house and to her bed where she covered her up and Annalise fell asleep.

"Annalise, wake up, Annalise," Annalise heard her mom call for her and woke up. She stood from her bed and walked over to her mirror with a long stretch and looked at herself in the mirror. She was normal again! The pajama set seemed to have grown with her, and Annalise laughed. She was an adult again! Thank the goddess. Annalise ran from her room downstairs and found her mother and grandmother in the kitchen cooking breakfast. She hugged them both and grabbed a piece of bacon.

"Good morning dear," Mom greeted.

"Mornin' lass," Lunasa, her grandmother, said to her. "What are you up to for today?"

Annalise hadn't had the chance to think about what she was going to do now that Snow was gone and her mother was safe. But there was something still bothering her. How come Dad didn't come that morning of Christmas? The last time he did, and he had taken her to the mansion in Scotland for a time. Lunasa hadn't even been around. Annalise looked at Lunasa and narrowed her eyes at her.

"Don't fash lass, I mean no harm. I really am your grandmother," she told Annalise and she felt at ease.

The battle had Annalise on edge, and she needed something to take her mind off it. She worked on her book, and for the next few days finished tying up loose ends and editing. It was published a month later, and while it was taking off, Annalise went in search of her own answers about Lachlan. She was no longer a child and could take a trip to Scotland on her own, so with the advance money she booked a flight to Scotland for her mom, grandma and her.

They landed in Edinburgh and took the four hours and fifty-six minutes to get to Skye. All for what? A chance that Lachlan was not dead centuries over? Annalise hoped that wasn't the case, and that Manna was right and that they would be reunited again. She wanted Manna as her daughter, and she wanted her with Lachlan.

Annalise went to the churches and looked through records; she went to libraries and found nothing about him. But knew the battle of Glendale was won because the fairy flag had been waived. But there was no mention of Lachlan at the battle. It was like he didn't exist in Otherworld. Annalise left the library disappointed.

"Why is this so important to you honey?" Mom asked her that night, in their hotel.

"Because, Lachlan is my mate. I cannot just leave him. I have to find him."

"We'll find him lassie," Annalise's grandmother assured her, but she wasn't so sure.

Annalise told them about her time in Otherworld, and Danu and Manna, and how Lachlan had forgotten about her and gained his memory back because of a ring he had given her.

"So you see, it is important that I find him," Annalise told them.

"You will," Mom said. "We just need a little more manpower. I think it's time to contact your father."

CHAPTER THIRTY-FOUR

Lachlan found himself in front of his parents' house. After going through the door that he guarded and walked through the time tunnel, Lachlan had been transported right outside his family home. He saw them now, sitting around the table eating, and his mother Cassie rose and turned with her plate and froze when she saw him.

Cassie dropped the plate she was holding and ran over to him and crushed him in a giant hug and sobbing. His father and sister, Riley, followed soon after. The only person who hadn't hugged him was Kieran who was standing in the distance with luggage in hand.

Lachlan walked over to him. "Where are you going?"

Kieran refused to look at him and went on his way without a word. Lachlan watched as he left, and Riley came over to him.

"He is mad, but he will be alright. He is going to Texas to open a second parlor," Riley signed.

Lachlan went about his time with his family and later that day, Lachlan poured over articles following Annalise on her career as an author. Her debut novel had been published early this year. Her biography had him snickering.

Annalise O'Callaghan is a new and upcoming romance author, selling millions of her debut novel within the first week, she is a national and international bestseller and a New York Times bestseller. When she is not writing, she is with her family walking around Seattle's night life. She loves dogs, the color purple and reads a lot. Like a lot a lot, seriously look at her book shelf. It's so huge! She is a freak!

So, Annalise was still in Seattle? Lachlan wondered if he should go after her or send her a message and have her come to him. He wasn't even sure she loved him still. They were mates, but that didn't mean a thing to him if she no longer loved him. Lachlan closed out of the computer and went in search of his father. There was one person who could talk to Annalise and knows where she is at: James O'Callaghan.

James looked at Lachlan as he sat on the other side of the room, he wanted to rage at the young man for hurting his daughter and not finding her when he had been back. James knew that Lachlan had been to Otherworld and that he had likely gone through one of the many time tunnels in Scotland. Yes, he knew that Lachlan was actually Llyr's son and an Unseelie prince. James wanted to be disgusted with the younger fae but unfortunately the boy really loved his daughter and James was a fae that just loved a sappy happily ever after.

"She is here in Scotland, at a hotel when I told her to take her new cottage for the month." James relaxed in his chair. "Of course, she is looking for you and has never stopped. I could tell you where she is, but I don't think you would like my terms. I am an entrepreneur after all."

"What are your terms? Not that I should be bargaining for Annalise's love, Mr. O'Callaghan," Lachlan told him.

James gave him a smile. "Simple, marry my girl, give me grand babies, and never hurt her again. Also, I would like your assistance with something as I could use your expertise on the matter."

"I will do what I can and you have nothing to worry about with me and Annalise," Lachlan agreed.

James extended his hands, and they shook completing their deal, and for the first time, the two courts came to an agreement on something, and that woke others who wanted them to stay separated.

CHAPTER THIRTY-FIVE

Lachlan drove to the cottage that James had given the address to. It was fairly large, had a porch made of stone, and a small garden in front. Lachlan drove into the driveway and parked the car behind a beautiful blue Impala. Lachlan got out of the car just as Annalise came out the door and froze on the porch. Her face went through a variety of emotions before she sprinted down the steps and into his arms. Lachlan kissed her deeply as he spun her around.

They walked into the cottage and shut the door.

"Where have you been?" Annalise said. "I looked for you everywhere."

Lachlan felt his heart flutter, she hadn't forgotten him as he had previously thought.

"I decided to go through the door I guarded, and the time tunnel. I thought you would return to me in Otherworld but unfortunately it never happened. You were missing, and I feared the worst," Lachlan said.

Annalise shuffled on her feet and looked down on them. "I am so sorry Lachlan, Joseph made me drink a potion from

Snow, and before I could say anything I was not in Otherworld anymore."

She told him about Danu and the goddess's odd request and she had been made to choose when she really didn't have a choice. Annalise told him about getting her book done so she could use her own money to come back to Scotland because she wanted to be the sole earner and get out from her father's shadow. She told him about her time as a child, and what it had felt like to go to school again and finding that she really liked it.

"None of it matters anymore, lass. We are together again and together to stay," Lachlan said.

Annalise agreed and pulled Lachlan into a kiss as she jumped into his arms and wrapped her legs around his waist and allowed him to carry her to the bedroom and the bed she had gotten from the mansion. Annalise laughed huskily as Lachlan lay her down, and started kissing her neck, collarbone and lifted her shirt up to free her breasts from her bra. He took one nipple into his mouth and took the other in his hand to play with it with his thumb rubbing the hard little nub while he suckled on the other and Annalise writhed beneath him. Lachlan popped her breast out of his mouth and unbuttoned her jeans and put his hand into her pants and under her panties to find her waiting wet canal. He inserted a finger, then two, and three and rubbed on the inside of her and Annalise wailed at the sensation of pleasure flowing through her like lightning.

He fucked her with his fingers until he had her coming so hard that she was screaming and whimpering. Lachlan withdrew his fingers and tugged down her pants and panties all in one swift motion and then rid himself of his clothing. Lachlan climbed on top of her and was inside of her in seconds closing the heat between them and entertaining them as they became one. The mating bond stretched, and everything seemed to blend together as Lachlan fucked her. The bond stretched more and more until it snapped with their orgasms and in its place, they felt such a completeness and their hearts were full. Annalise was Lachlan's star to his moon. She was his, his and no one else's.

Later that night, Lachlan zipped Annalise to the fairy pools where they made love in the water and then walked under the moonlight and stars. It was a pleasant night, not too cold and not too warm, just right. For them it was a perpetual springtime here at the Fairy pools just for them when they came to the pools. This was because of their fae magic, and loving bond. It would forever bloom with flowers and warmth whenever Lachlan and Annalise appeared, congratulating them for their connection.

"Oh how sweet," a voice said in the darkness.

Annalise and Lachlan found Joseph walking out of the dark with a gun raised at Annalise. Lachlan stepped in front of Annalise just as Joseph shot the gun hitting him in his chest. Lachlan fell onto one knee and clutched his chest. His wings burst forth from his back, and Annalise came forward and blasted him with a ball of green and knocked him to the ground the gun flying through the air and landing into the fairy pool.

Joseph stood and wiped the blood from his lip. "You bitch!" He drew a knife and went after her and this time Annalise got ahold of his arms and red light emanated from her hands and wrapped around Joseph.

Joseph stumbled back and looked at Annalise shocked. "How did you…What is happening?" He began to grow old and then turned to dust just as Snow had.

Annalise stepped back and looked at her hands. Just what in the hell was that, and had she really just killed Joseph Declan? Annalise looked at Lachlan and ran to him just as the bullet pushed itself out and Lachlan fell to the ground out cold. Annalise grabbed him and checked his pulse and then called the police when she noticed he was barely breathing.

Annalise watched as Lachlan was wheeled into the back and away from her to be prepped for surgery, they feared that the bullet had punctured a lung and needed to get him in as fast as they could. She tried not to freak out, and was relieved when her mom, Lunasa, and her dad showed up at the hospital not moments after she had called them. Annalise's mom and grandmother took her into their arms as her dad went off to find Murdoch, Lachlan's dad. They came back an hour later with Cassie and Riley in tow but not Kieran, he was missing.

"Where is Kieran?" Annalise asked Cassie.

"He left, was very upset he was at Lachlan. We all were, but we were just glad that he came back when he did. Kieran was going to Texas anyhow, he wanted to open another Sky Ink in Fort Worth and investigate what happened to my side of the family at my request," Cassie explained.

Annalise nodded and couldn't't blame Kieran for being angry, but someone had to get a hold of him and tell him that Lachlan was in the hospital and likely will fight for his life. Annalise got his number from Riley and tried calling him but it simply went straight to voicemail.

"Kieran this is Annalise when you get this message please call me back, Lachlan has been shot," Annalise told him and then hung up the phone and gave it back to her dad.

"He didn't answer," she told all of them and their shoulders slumped.

It was hours before they knew anything about Lachlan, and when the surgeon came out, they could hardly believe their luck that the surgery was finally over.

"How is he?" Murdoch asked the surgeon

"He pulled through Dr. Mac. He will be fine, no other

damage than through and through, no perforations or anything."

Annalise smiled and thanked the goddess that he came out alright. She didn't know what she would have done if he hadn't.

"Thank you, Hank," Murdoch said to the surgeon and looked at them with a warm smile.

There was something different about Murdoch, he didn't look as full of life as he did once before and seemed to have lost some weight. Annalise wondered if maybe he was feeling bad. She approached him.

"I hope you are well Murdoch, I am sorry about Lachlan."

"I am fine, just a bit of a cold unfortunately but I will be on the mend soon," he said.

Annalise nodded and went in search of Cassie and Riley. She found them signing to each other vigorously, and Riley stomped her foot. Likely something that Cassie shot down. Annalise walked over to them, and they talked for a good hour until they were allowed to go back and see Lachlan. Annalise was the last one back as she wanted his family to share in his recovery and see that he was alright. They needed that because they nearly lost their son to death again, this time for real. Annalise walked over to him lying in his bed and he lifted his arms and she embraced him. He was his spring and she was his summer.

CHAPTER THIRTY-SIX

Late that night Lachlan woke her up with a crazy idea.

"Why don't we get married here?"

"Here? Lachlan this is a hospital," Annalise said.

"So? It has a beautiful garden and I can do it after I have had physical therapy," Lachlan explained.

Annalise laughed. "Lachlan they aren't going to let us get married here at the hospital."

He winked at her. "Don't worry, I will take care of everything my love."

Three days later they were married with Murdoch officiating and hospital staff watching Annalise come down the hallway in a wedding gown her mom had worn at her wedding. It fit snuggly, hugged her hips and flowed out in beautiful ripples with embroidered flowers, butterflies of different colors and slippers to match. In her ears, she wore tear drop pearl earrings, and a pearl necklace which had the feather that Lachlan had left when he had gone to Otherworld. Lachlan told her it was meant to send her back home but now the magic lay dormant and unused. It had failed the minute that Joseph had put the potion in Annalise's mouth.

Lachlan wore his kilt and regalia from his time in the military and looked so handsome with his long black hair tied into a braid down his back. He turned to face her with a smile and reached out his hand. Annalise took it and joined him in that hallway hand in hand forever amongst the stars.

They ate a dinner from the hospital made for them by the staff and talked of the future. She was now Mrs. Macleod and Manna would be born. In fact, she hoped real soon. Annalise left Lachlan to rest, and found her mother and grandmother looking out the window at the falling snow.

"Annalise dear, how did you defeat Snow and Joseph again?" her mom asked her.

Annalise shrugged. "I don't know, it just happened, they turned to dust and disappeared like they never existed. My hands were a blood red and so was the spell."

Lunasa looked at Annalise and shook her head. "You must not use that type of magic, it is evil."

Annalise looked down. "I didn't know."

"Of course you didn't which is why I am telling you now girl, don't use that kind of magic unless it's an absolute emergency. That magic is evil and consumes even the gentlest souls," Lunasa explained.

Annalise nodded and vowed to never use that type of magic again. She had actually killed two people. She was feeling the guilt for that already, but this was even worse. Annalise had used magic that Snow would have used on her, and now she was no longer perfect.

Lachlan was released two weeks later after healing a lot better than they thought he would. He took Annalise to Edinburgh on their honeymoon and then on to Ireland and Dublin. Annalise had never been so happy, and the guilt that she felt was suddenly gone and she forgave herself and vowed to never do that again.

A month passed and Annalise was not feeling herself so

she made an appointment at the doctor for fear it was the flu. She came out of that hospital with a smile on her face, and her hand on her stomach and she told Lachlan the moment she got home. They were pregnant and Manna would finally be here.

EPILOGUE

KIERAN UN-BOARDED THE PLANE IN FORT WORTH LOVE FIELD and called the taxi. He saw that he had several messages from his family, but the one that stood out was Annalise's call. He clicked the voicemail and went to listen but the taxi came and he had to quickly get into it before another person went for it as they did the other taxis. Kieran had picked out a quaint apartment on the west side of Fort Worth a little further away from the stockyards, but he was never one to mix business with his daily life.

Kieran paid the driver when they pulled up to the Rose apartment complex. He looked around and found that it looked nothing like the picture Kieran had seen previously. Perhaps the current owners had poor taste? Or maybe they didn't care about the property and its tenants. The reviews said it was an outstanding place to live, but the state of it now had Kieran questioning it. He walked into the leasing office and stopped when he saw the landlord. Her long blond hair bouncing as she walked into the office, her lithe body perfect in every way. By the way she held herself, he could tell she was a powerful woman. She wore a pantsuit that hugged her every curve. Kieran's cock made it uncomfortable to move and he had to adjust myself. Why did she make him feel this way? Kieran didn't know her, she was practically a stranger until today. He walked over to her and smiled and extended his hand.

"Hello, I am Kieran Macleod."

Lightning Source UK Ltd.
Milton Keynes UK
UKHW010318140223
416945UK00007B/818